THE STORY OF LAND AND SEA

KATY SIMPSON SMITH

ISIS
LARGE
PRINT

First published in Great Britain 2015
by
The Borough Press
An imprint of HarperCollins*Publishers*

First Isis Edition
published 2016
by arrangement with
HarperCollins*Publishers*

*A catalogue record for this book is available
from the British Library.*

ISBN 978–1–78541–247–9 (hb)
ISBN 978–1–78541–253–0 (pb)

Published by
F. A. Thorpe (Publishing)
Anstey, Leicestershire

Set by Words & Graphics Ltd.
Anstey, Leicestershire
Printed and bound in Great Britain by
T. J. International Ltd., Padstow, Cornwall

This book is printed on acid-free paper

FOR
MY FATHER

There is a land of pure delight
Where saints immortal reign;
Infinite day excludes the night,
And pleasures banish pain.

There everlasting spring abides,
And never-withering flowers;
Death like a narrow sea divides
This heavenly land from ours . . .

But timorous mortals start and shrink
To cross this narrow sea,
And linger shivering on the brink,
And fear to launch away . . .

Could we but climb where Moses stood
And view the landscape o'er,
Not Jordan's stream, nor death's cold flood,
Should fright us from the shore.

ISAAC WATTS

Part One

1793

CHAPTER
ONE

On days in August when sea storms bite into the North Carolina coast, he drags a tick mattress into the hall and tells his daughter stories, true and false, about her mother. The wooden shutters clatter, and Tabitha folds blankets around them to build a softness for the storm. He always tells of their courting days, of her mother's shyness. She looked like a straight tall pine from a distance; only when he got close could he see her trembling.

"Was she scared?"

"Happy," John says. "We were both happy."

He watches Tab pull the quilt up to her chin, though even the storm can't blow away the heat of summer. She is waiting to hear his secrets. But it is hard to describe how it feels to stand next to someone you love on the shore at dusk. He didn't have to see Helen to know she was there. Something in her body pulled at something in his, across the humid air between them.

"When you're older," he says, and she nods, familiar with this response.

"Why don't you ever tell about the ship?" she asks. "All the things you must have seen with her."

He looks down the hall at the shadows whipping across the slats and holds a finger to his lips. "Can you hear any birds?"

Tab slips into the kitchen for an end of bread in the darkness of the storm. She will keep asking him until he tells her. In the quilts again, she tucks close against him. As the wind rattles through the palmettos and the rain melts the window glass, John sings one of his sailing tunes to soothe her. Tabitha calls out, "Louder!" and he rises to his feet, unsteady on the mattress, waving his browned hands to the melody. His voice carries through the quiet rooms.

He doesn't tell her about the day he walked Helen onto a ship with a captain he knew from his pirate days, one small bag between them, and they curled beneath the gunwale until the frigate had pulled its anchor and filled its sails and was tacking through the shoals out of the bay. Only when the mate gave a wink did they stand — Helen wobbling, clutching him for support, laughing like a girl, her hair pulled by the wind — and watch the town slowly shrink until it was no bigger than a piece of driftwood, a brown and gold splotch against the shore.

He doesn't tell Tab about the beauty of her mother as she struggled to find some dignity on a vessel made seaworthy by its layers of filth. A year they were on that ship, married and her with the seed of a child in her by the end, and Helen transformed from some kind of pristine saint to the sunburned woman who tucked her skirts up to scrub the deck with him, who wrapped her hands around his when he fished off the side of the ship in the evenings. Could such a woman really have come

4

back to live in the world again? The curses she learned, the brownness of her skin, the way her laughter got louder, as though to compete with the waves.

Who will Tabitha be when she becomes a woman?

After the storm, they walk to the shore to see what the ocean has relinquished. Fallen leaves and branches line the way. Half buried in sand is the cracked husk of a horseshoe crab. Tab scrapes her fingernails along its papery hide and leaves it for the waves to eat again.

It is 1793, and they live in Beaufort in a four-room house, two above and two below, built by a childless cousin in the lumber trade who was killed by a falling pine. One block north of the water, three blocks east of the store where John sells sundries. In the summer the doors hang open, front and back, and a salt breeze snakes through the hall. In thunder, the windows clamor. The girl's room upstairs faces the marsh and smells of fish in the morning and in the afternoon catches all the southern light. On moonless nights she sleeps with her father for fear of riding witches.

Mrs. Foushee leads the school in town, where children, mostly girls, pass time if their mothers are not birthing or poor. Their small hands rub the grooves in wooden tables and slip between the pages of spelling books. The letters dance for them. Mrs. Foushee is a soldier's wife and sleeps in his bed and listens to him remember the Revolution, but in the schoolroom she wearies of duty. For most of the day she sits, and has the children bring their work to her. She lets them out early or fails to call them back from dinner. She idles with her embroidery, sucks on candies, and sometimes dozes. The girls creep to her chair and watch, some fondling the pink brocade of her skirts, others plucking strands of silver hair fallen on her bosom and setting fire to them for the smell of it. Her eyelids droop; her mouth, still full in middle age, hangs limp. She taught Tab's mother too.

At nine, Tabitha knows her alphabet and most small words and can count up shillings and pence on her fingers. She can play three melodies on the church organ, and if taken to France, she could ask for bread and water. This is also the bulk of Mrs. Foushee's knowledge. Most days Tab lets the woman sleep and the other pupils plait their hair. She stares instead through the open door to the ocean, which she knows better than she knows her mother.

The town is older now, in the way that some towns age; most of the young people have grown up. Some went to war and died, and others took their small inheritances and moved to Wilmington or Raleigh. When John's cousin was felled, no other relative would return to take his house in Beaufort. But John had a wife with child, and the sea was no place for a baby. The remaining families in town live in a slender band along the ocean, just a few streets deep. Those with money have collected the surrounding fields for rice or lumber, and beyond the plantations, marsh and forest unroll inland. A single road through this wilderness binds Beaufort to New Bern. The town seems to be slowly cutting itself off.

Tab doesn't know many children. There are Mrs. Foushee's pupils, some ragged boys that belong to poor farmers on the edge of town, and the children of slaves, whom she can spot in the fields by their smallness. They are half steps in the long rows of bent bodies. They rarely come into town, and when they do, they don't look up. Tab knows her father has some acquaintances among the slaves, but she doesn't think this is so unusual. Silent threads run in all directions through the town, and Tab is not blind. He never brings them to meet her, though, or speaks to them outright. Tab doesn't know the rules about this. One woman comes into the store sometimes with eggs to sell and a little boy by her side, the same size as Tab. John looks at them hard, and the woman looks hard back, but their words are mostly ordinary. The boy tries to touch everything in the store. He feels the barrels and hoes and sacks of dried corn like they were all silk. He smiles at Tab, as though he knew everything that she knew. But Tab is not his friend, nor is she the friend of the powdery girls in Mrs. Foushee's schoolroom or the boys who throw rocks on the edge of town. She has her father.

Summer mornings when Mrs. Foushee is ill or Tabitha's blood is jumping, the girl walks to the marshes along the waterfront and swims with slow strokes to the sandbar between the sound and the ocean. She lies on the grit, limbs spread, fingers and toes burying themselves in warmth. Eyes closed, she sees battles fought on water. Ships — French, British, and ghost — with cannon booming and flags snapping, their precarious shapes lit by the piling clouds of summer. Bursts of gunfire paint the sunset.

She digs channels by the shore to let the water in and builds moats and islands of defense. Oak leaves pummel each other, and moss bits leap into the shallow salt water, bodies flung out to sea. Cannonball pebbles land on the leaves, dooming them, sending their wreckage to the depths for stone crabs to scuttle over. There are no mercies in this play.

The battle over, the leaves drowned, Tabitha searches for treasure. She has sewn large pockets onto the front of her dresses to carry home the pink-eared shells and dry fish bones. She used to leave her findings in a pit at the center of the island, but a storm scattered them all. Now she takes them with her. Her bedroom becomes wild with the ocean's debris. She steps on something sharp and pulls broken brass from a sucking cove where the water seeps in. A shard of armor, she assumes. Her father, not knowing the best thing for her, lets her wander.

At dusk, the marshes turn purple and heavy. From the sandbar, the dimpled muck of the shore smooths over. The reeds quiver with bitterns. A strand of clouds sinks to the west, blanketing the last pink edge. When Tab slips into the dark water, silver-brushed, a burst of herring gulls cries out, winging up. She opens her eyes beneath the surface, letting her body float, her hair drift. Her shift gathers water. A dark small shape passes below her, and she lifts her head up fast, gasping. A strand of hair slides into her mouth when she sucks in air. She begins to kick and reach and in a few minutes is ankle-deep again in brown grime, her hands reaching for stalks to pull her feet from the mud. Her pockets still hang heavy with treasure. Her wet legs collect sand all the way home.

On Sundays, Asa comes in a brown suit. Though he and John rarely speak of Helen, Asa's green eyes remind both men of her. He carries a book in his hands and waits in the hall for his granddaughter. John asks him to sit, and he shakes his head, staring out the open back door. John asks how his trees grow, and Asa says, "Passable." John leaves his father-in-law standing there and retires to the parlor to read the weekly papers. Later in the morning, John will wander down to the harbor and greet the ships that dock, looking for old friends amidst the crews. Tabitha comes downstairs in a pinching dress, her only one without pockets, and slips her hand into her grandfather's without a smile. She says good-bye to John, and they walk the five blocks to church. The building is brick and stands uneasily on stone pillars. Asa is Anglican, but Anglicanism is dying out, and his old church was taken over by Methodists. Most of the Anglicans retreated to this smaller chapel, where they have realigned with the Episcopalians. He cannot keep track of the names of Christianity. People are still searching for what they used to know. Here there is no stained glass and the pine floorboards are warping. The church does have a little square tower and a cupola with a bell, but from the street one can see they rest at a tilt.

Sitting in the pew with his granddaughter, he wishes for cushions. When he was a boy, services were held in the courthouse; he had a gilded Bible and his bottom could rest on a pillow while he listened to the Lord's word. But now the sons are moving away, leaving their fathers' farms, and churches are left wanting. The town talked of building a canal to join the two rivers on the way to New Bern so boats could pass with goods, but the men who had the funds were loath to spend them, and Beaufort — which could have controlled the inland trade — became stagnant, and then began to shrink. The goodness in the world he knew has contracted; the common feeling they had under royal rule has turned to self-interest. Men grasp at money instead of virtue. All the men he knows are common bandits. He hopes God is watching.

Tabitha, who swings her legs when she is forced to sit, kicks the back of his ankle, sending his leg knocking into the pew in front of him. The minister pauses, and resumes. Asa pinches her wrist and glares.

The Reverend Solomon Halling stands at the pulpit and makes gentle flourishes with his hands. The pulpit is made of pine, carved with a large flower and several smaller flowers, which might also be four-petaled crosses. Asa always wonders if a woman made it. Halling comes down from New Bern a few times a year; mostly, they listen to vestrymen or sing songs amongst themselves. The congregation has been halved in recent years. Instead of gathering at the front, they keep their family seats, the spaces between them widening. Halling reminds the listeners what it is to be

Episcopalian, that it is merely Anglicanism without the thrall to monarchy. A few women fidget in the pews. A child sneezes and then begins to cry, so Halling shifts to a hymn. The people stand, and those who earn their living by the sea rub their woolen vests. They blush to hear the sound of their own voices.

During the hymns, Asa always hears his absent daughter. The clarity of her tone once reminded him of his wickedness. He is one of the men who comes to church to punish himself, though of course there is pleasure in this penance. When he glances down at his granddaughter, she seems like a stranger.

After the parishioners have offered prayer and been exhorted to goodness and donation, the Reverend Dr. Halling stands on the sagging steps and shakes their hands. On this Sunday, Asa gives him a half pound for the new church and pushes Tabitha forward to shake his hand. Though new to the parish, the minister is worn, with graying locks frizzed around his shoulders and dull brown eyes. He was a surgeon during the war, and after the piecing together of men's bodies, the care of their souls has finally tired him. When he smiles, his teeth catch on his lip, so he is ever adjusting his mouth to bring it to stasis.

"My granddaughter," Asa says, his hand tight on her shoulder. Tabitha wipes her palms on her dress. "She and her father are wayward in faith."

Halling nods. "Has she her own hymnal?" He slips back into the church, upsetting a flock of older women who croon after him, and in a few moments returns with a tattered brown book and hands it to Asa. "Mostly Watts," he says.

"I fear I am her only guidance," Asa says.

Halling shakes his head and holds his hand out flat, palm up. "You forget the Lord." He turns back to the crowd, which is still absorbing the presence of ordination.

Tab pulls on her grandfather's hand. The tides are rolling out, and she can smell the fishermen's catch, can hear the gasping holes the crabs make in the sand.

Asa holds the book on the walk home, wondering about the rightness of letting a heathen child possess the word of God. Where is the purpose in watering fallow fields? He wishes there was a minister year-round. His God is a fickle one, and Asa does not always comprehend the trajectories of the lives around him. He looks only for evidence of justice. He looks for reasons why he has been so punished.

In the summer of 1783, his daughter, Helen, returned to him after a year of dissipation. She had been seduced by John, a common soldier, married without her father's blessing, abandoned her inheritance to set sail with the soldier on a black-flagged ship, and had come home with a belly full of child. Asa waited for God's fist to fall on her husband. As John built new shelves in the merchant's store in which he had purchased a share, Asa waited for the hammer to slip and strike John's hand, the board to crack upon his head. During August storms when John and Helen would stand by the water, arms entwined, bodies warm for each other, Asa waited for the swells to pull John in,

12

leaving his daughter alone on the shore. He wanted her back, untouched. He watched as they fixed up the house left to them by John's cousin, painting it fresh white, filling it with oddments from the sea, tilling the grit outside for potatoes and corn. He never saw them sad or thoughtful. Their joy was the devil's mark.

When her time came in October, a storm swept in from the southeast and whipped up the waves. Asa wanted to carry his daughter inland for the birth, to protect her among the trees, but she clung to the house she and John had adorned. If her child was going to know the world, she wanted it to know all, the gale and breeze alike. Despite Helen's requests, Asa refused to pray for her. He had prayed for his own wife during a similar storm, during the same mortal passage, and she had been taken. He could not pray again, not in the same way. But he came to her when she began to labor, and he waited with her, as he had not waited with his wife, and the whole scene was a mirror to him, as if God was showing him what he missed the first time.

He and John carried water for the midwife, tore scraps of linen, carried more water. They did not speak, and when John reached for his arm, Asa pulled away. Neither man should have been a witness, but Asa insisted; he would no longer let women control this moment. They stood in the corner of the room with their arms crossed, eyes on the floor. Looking over the shoulder of the midwife, whose hands were busy with cloth and water and touch, Helen begged her father to tell her if this was how it usually happened, and whether her mother had felt this way. She was a child again, and needed his voice. He nodded and said everything was just as it should be, though he had not seen his wife in labor and wouldn't know what was ordinary, but yes, no reason to worry, and surely Helen had the strength for it. But she was not listening.

As the storm tunneled through the streets of Beaufort, an infant arrived: red and angry and screaming over the howls of wind. The midwife placed the child in a basket while she pressed vinegar rags to the mother's wounds. John and Asa stood beyond the cast of candlelight, staring at the weeds of hair pressed against Helen's white cheeks, listening to the thinness of her breaths. She began to weep.

Asa left in the morning, after the squall had blown away north, and took his daughter's body with him. He said he would come back for the living child.

When Asa goes to church, he carries a list of sins in his heart, waiting for forgiveness.

Summer blends into fall. Yellow warblers and flocks of bobolinks arrive on the salt marshes, and sandpipers poke along the mudflats, watching for holes. In the forests around Beaufort, the sumacs turn fiery red, and the wild grapes grow purple and fat. By October, the evenings are finally cool.

Tab cannot sleep the night before her tenth birthday. She has a rasp in her throat that feels like dry biscuits. Kneeling instead by the window, wrapped in her mother's shawl, she traces patterns in the stars, fingering out dogs and chariots on the frosting pane, her chin propped on the sill. She closes her eyes only to imagine the model ship that might appear wrapped in brown paper at dawn. It has three masts and is made of thin paneling stained nut brown. Its sails are coarse linen, and a tiny wheel spins behind the mizzen-mast. Netting hangs along its decks. On the starboard side, a small trapdoor is cut into the planks that you can lift and peer through into the hold. She would fill its empty belly with detritus. Acorns, feathers, moss. She saw it in a shop in New Bern on their last visit there to purchase fabric for the store. Tab made a point of standing still before the window until her father, strides ahead, missed her and turned.

"Ships, eh?" he said, and tugged gently at the back collar of her dress.

"Tell me something again," she said, and as they walked away from the shining toy boat, he began another tale about her mother, and she knew that he had known, that he had seen the want in her eyes and understood.

In the carriage home, her father hid a large package beneath the seat and winked at her. All she had to do was wait for it to come into her hands.

John sleeps sometimes in his bedroom across the slanting hall from Tabitha, but there are nights when he can smell his wife's body in the bed and he takes his blankets downstairs. He finds a space among the furniture in the parlor — pieces given to his wife by her parents, and to them by their parents — on rugs bartered or stolen from vessels he has hailed on the saltwater rises, below paintings of flat faces and flat children holding shrunken lambs, between cabinets of glass bottles, Spanish gold, musket balls, a rusted crown, bells. The remnants of booty that are now only treasure to a child. There is a mirror in this room with a peeling silver back, and sometimes in its spaces, Helen appears, wearing blue, her dark hair in braids behind her head, curls sprouting. Her green eyes depth-colored. He talks to her here, or he is afraid, the way her eyes follow him, and he takes his blankets into the hearth room, where pots with grease line the fireplace and shelves hold dry goods, bolts of fabric, sacks of meal. This is where he keeps the store's excess. When customers ask for mustard seed, he brings them here, or says it must be delivered special and so gets a few pence extra. They have never wanted, he and his child. And still her phantom moves through the rooms, reminding him of what they lack.

The night before Tab's tenth birthday, John sleeps on the low green sofa in the parlor. It faces a portrait of his wife's grandmother as a girl, who looked nothing like her, so he can imagine that he has loved someone else entirely.

He wakes in the middle of the night, as he often does, to her voice calling him. He walks out of the house, across the dirt road, and down to the marsh, where he closes his eyes and lets the wind pulse at him; through the harshness of brine and shore decay, he catches again the blooming smell of her. He has fallen asleep here before, but it scared his daughter not to find him in the house, so he's more careful now. The grief, besides, has waned to washes of melancholy, impressions connected to no specific hurt but to the awareness of a constant. He is in no pain but the pain of the living.

The frogs are calling in the darkness, hungry for rain. If flocks of birds migrate by the stars, perhaps the spaces between those points of light are not blackness but the bodies of birds; perhaps there is in fact no absence of light in the sky, only stars and birds. When he walks back toward the house, he sees a small shape against the upstairs window. The head of his sleeping daughter, pressed against the glass. So there are nights when neither of them can sleep in beds. This is what she has done to them.

John comes from no family of his own, so every turn of love and lack of love surprises him. His parents were dead before he knew them, and he was raised by kin who had kin of their own to cherish. He was caught between families, on a rural farm, with ties to no one. When he first left for the sea, his mother's second cousin wrapped him up a sack of crackers and was in the fields again before John was half down the road. When he came back as a soldier, there was no embrace. He wonders if fatherhood is easy to men who had fathers.

In October, meadowlarks descend on the shores and islands, and mockingbirds brighten the early days of fall with song. The morning raucousness is a sign that Tabitha's birthday is nearing, that time is passing. These days, when John sees her ramble into the house, mud-splattered, with bursting pockets and hair escaping from its pins, he senses he has not done right.

He has not been a mother and father to her. She is a woman after all — if not yet, then soon — and he has allowed her to grow sexless and wild. He should ask Mrs. Foushee over more often, or Mrs. Randolph, his father-in-law's housekeeper. They could show her how to make tea.

A few weeks ago, they traveled in the trap to New Bern, and while Tab peeked in shop windows and pitched stones at the governor's palace, he bought supplies for the store. Fabric, soaps, medicines. Rubbing the cloth between his fingers, he had chosen some simple linens for his customers in Beaufort, stripes and ticking, linsey-woolsey, a heavy damask. But there had been a silk that shone. Blue, with vine patterns in pink and green. The polish of it felt like the skin of his wife. He bought yardage for a ten-year-old girl, had it wrapped in brown paper, and they rode home in the carriage the following day. She had seen his proud grin. Fathering had no end. There was no stage at which you could no longer improve. They rode back through swamps and prairies and wooded hammocks, and as John guided their horses over the puddled roads, he watched sidelong as his daughter slumped and slept, her face against the carriage side.

He returns to the house, mud on his bare soles, and as the sky turns from purple to gray, he begins a pot of hominy in the hearth, spicing it with old fat and pepper.

She is asleep against the sill, her breath fogging the window in steady rhythm. The moon sheen in the sky

18

begins to dim. Her head rests on one cocked arm, pressed against the chilled glass. Her knees are bent beneath her, and one hand curls into an empty cup. She is dreaming of water; always dreaming of water.

Below, John stirs the hominy. He pours a spoon of fat into the iron pot and watches it ease across the corn. When Tab was younger, his wife's father loaned them Mrs. Randolph, who cooked proper in the kitchen near the well. But like all grown women, she had reminded him of Helen. Now the outbuildings are home to the roaming chickens that Tab won't let him catch, so he buys dead ones at market. Sometimes she cooks, sometimes he. He sits back on his heels, his hands around the ladle, and stares into the fire. It moves like a woman.

The musky smell of the fat climbs the stairs, and Tab is awake. Her face contracts into the beginnings of a cry. Her body hurts from sleeping against the wall, though sometimes this pain is better than waking up in a soft bed. The bottom of the window has frosted over from her breath. To the south are no warm yellows, only a dull gray that lightens when she turns her head away and then back. When an egret bobs in slow flight beyond the far marsh, pale white against pale gray, she remembers it's her birthday.

Tabitha comes downstairs in bare feet, her head feeling crowded with sharp rocks. She follows the scent of breakfast. John is kneeling with the ladle by the hearth. She leans against the doorpost and closes her eyes. John turns at her small sounds, and smiles. "Look at this stranger, a girl of ten. What does she fancy?"

"Hominy, please," she says, "and pudding." Tab slips into a chair and rests her head upon the table, which smells of salt and old grease.

"You could have stayed in bed," John says.

"I don't feel very well," Tab says.

John spoons the mush into silver bowls that bear the scrolled stamp of his wife's family, and comes to feel the girl's forehead and cheeks. "From sleeping by the window, is my reckoning." He offers her a spoon. "Warmth will help."

She eats while he draws an image of the day. He proposes a walk along the shore, and when she asks about Mrs. Foushee, he says today is for the two of them. Not even Asa can intrude. He even hints at a gift. She smiles at the thought of the wooden ship with the trapdoor on its deck. They love each other extra much for being only two. Her mother is a phantom she thinks of fondly, like some angel from the Milton her father reads aloud, but she cannot imagine her in this house, her limbs moving in this salted air. Just as she would not like God to live in her bedroom, her mother too is better bodyless.

Her mouth dries and a bubble lodges in her throat. She swallows several times, then burps. She looks at her father, as if for an answer. A sea is rising in her. She stands quickly and moves to the corner, where the heat of grits and sharp stomach water floods through her mouth. A rusting thread runs through the puddle on the floor.

John brings her back to her chair. He dips a rag in the basin of water and stretches it across her forehead, then takes another to wipe up the vomit and blood. He begins to sing a shanty. When her breathing is calm, he carries her upstairs to bed. She opens her eyes as he lays her on the sheet.

"We'll fetch Dr. Yarborough," he says, and stands there, arms hanging, until she falls asleep again.

When she wakes in the falling of the afternoon, four uneasy men are in her room. One leans against the base of her bed, one sits and holds her wrist lightly, two stand in the corner, gray haired, murmuring. Her back is clenching in pain, as if something is growing there. There are splinters in her head. She cannot pull her wrist away from the hand that holds it. The room looks watery. The seated man in spectacles releases her and rubs the side of his nose with his finger. He looks at the man standing at her feet, who, when he moves, takes the shape of her father. One of them says, "We can only wait now," and the other three men nod.

John leads the doctor out, and Asa brings the vestryman closer. He does not speak clearly, but she thinks he is blessing her. Though ten years old, she feels very young and is wise enough to know that death only comes to mothers, and this she plans never to be. When she blinks, the vestryman is soaked, as though her grandfather rescued him from the sea, and the marsh grasses cling to his bald skull. His eyes are the sockets of a pecked-out butterfish. His wrists end in squids. When she opens her eyes again, the room is black and empty. Her pillow is damp, and her knees ache. She pulls her legs to her chest to stretch them and in this ball of pain, she rolls herself to her floor. She knows the thud will wake her father, but from here she can see the moon, pulling and pushing the ocean, kneading it along the shore. She hears its voices and is calm on the coolness of the boards.

When John appears in the doorway, she asks him to leave her where she is.

When the sun rises, they are both on the bedroom floor. Tab is dreaming of underwater. She wakes and remembers all the hurt, which pierces her back and knees and makes her muscles quiver and her stomach riot. She crawls downstairs and into the remnants of her mother's garden and heaves blood again.

Asa finds her here, curled around a cabbage rose.

In bed again, wrapped in quilts too heavy to slip from, Tabitha hears the men below. She feels as if she is fainting, though she knows that if she were, she wouldn't be able to tell. In the spaces between knowing and not knowing, she sees her mother sitting on the side of the bed, a leg swinging below the mattress. Tab knows one of them must be ten years old. They both have dark curls twisted up and away from pale faces. Her mother's eyes are green, and Tab thinks her own are brown. Her mother's dress is white and thin. She reaches out for it, but her fingers are weighed down by the quilt. Her mother is not smiling; if this were a dream, her mother would be smiling, so this must be real. When she moves her eyes, her head spasms, so she closes them and enjoys the feel of her mother's weight on the side of her bed.

"She'll be better cared for at Long Ridge," Asa says. Asa named his turpentine plantation after his own wife died in giving birth and a farmer told him land unnamed brought the devil walking. It lies a mile east of town, a white house planted between acres of pines to the north and a lawn that slopes south to the water. A white house in the midst of nothing.

"She stays." John is not looking at Asa but at the waving rushes on the shore below town. They toss around and tell you nothing of the wind's direction.

On the sofa, Asa crosses a knee and lets his hand fall on the side table, which holds remnants of his daughter's life. A pincushion, a hair catch, a miniature on ivory that he once thought was being painted for him, before he knew his daughter had fallen in love. With his thumb, he presses the pins in to their heads. "I do this for the child, you understand," he says. "I have no intent to punish you."

John turns from the window and listens for any upstairs sound. "It wasn't the sea that killed Helen."

"No," Asa says, "but it was you, and that amounts to the same." He knows this isn't true as he is saying it, but it feels good to cause pain, and it isn't wholly false.

"Then despise Tab too." John walks to the side table and places a finger on the pincushion so that Asa draws his hand back into his lap. "You are welcome to stay, but my daughter will be with me. Dr. Yarborough is tending her, and if there's any danger, it will be the same there as it is here."

Asa stands. "And what of your daughter's soul? Will you let her go to the next world without a minister present?" He almost says, *Won't you pray for her?* In blaming John, he is only blaming himself.

John pauses at the stairs, his back to Asa. "Tab isn't going anywhere. And if their souls are what they live on by, then I am in keeping of them."

Mrs. Foushee comes with a lemon cake, but she doesn't ask to see the girl. John guides her to the parlor, where she sits and waits politely until John stands again and fetches a knife and two plates. She cuts thick slices.

"You know how much I care for your family," she says. Before she married, Mrs. Foushee had taught Helen her letters. Though the teacher had left her stamp on most of Beaufort's youth, she and Helen had been close. She had supported John's cause when they were first courting. But like Helen's other friends, she has drifted away since Helen's death. She is thinking of this now, looking around the messy parlor. "I've tried to keep an eye on Tabitha, but she's an independent sort, isn't she? I don't mean to neglect her, or you, certainly. I'm sure you'll let me know if there's any way I can be of service. If the girl needs some womanly guidance." She has finished her slice and eyes the rest of the lemon cake on the side table.

John asks if she'd like some more.

"I couldn't possibly. It's really for Tabitha, bless her. You know girls this age are always getting ill — I think it's part of growing. Soon she'll fill out into quite a lady, you'll see." As though she were brushing away crumbs, Mrs. Foushee smooths her own ample sides, demonstrating what exactly a woman looks like. "Her mother was the same. Little complaints." Despite having a husband at home, she harbors an affection for the young men of the town that is not entirely maternal. She misses the men who were garrisoned in Beaufort during the war — William Dennis, Daniel Foot, Colonel Easton — and who have set up lives in more prosperous places. Of all the soldiers, John is the only one who stayed. Loss has a way of paralyzing even the brave. She reaches out now and pats his knee. "We'll see her through it, don't worry yourself."

When she leaves, John is grateful for the quiet. In the first few years after Helen's death, he thought he might be lonely, but Tab is all he wants in the way of company. He carries a slice of cake upstairs, but his daughter is sleeping, her mouth open.

Yarborough returns in the afternoon and places his cool hands on the girl's body. She is asleep again, though there is no restfulness about her. John sits on a rush-bottomed chair in the corner and watches the doctor's face. Yarborough opens her mouth, looks at her tongue. He peels back her eyelids, which are still and pliant. He rubs his fingers along the pale insides of her arms, looking for the blood within. He examines her as a child picks at his supper, knowing already what is there.

When the doctor turns, John is shaking his head. "Yellow fever," Yarborough says. "She may improve. The likelihood, indeed, is that she will improve. But the danger is in the lapsing. Steady rest, fluids, quiet."

"Nothing to be done?" John asks.

"Prayer," the doctor says. "The minister from New Bern returns on his circuit tomorrow. You might have him stop in with a word."

John is left alone in his daughter's bedroom. He remembers being her age, being God-loving and prayerful. Believing in a goodness without end, and wrath for the undeserving. Even aboard ship, his cannon pointed at another crew, his sins could be laundered. But in the birthing of his child, he had forgotten to call out to the Lord. He only saw his wife, her belly, his infant. And without his prayers, she had been taken. This began his acquaintance with God as a vengeful child who, if ignored, will snatch his favorite toy away. So John offered him nothing. Unable to blame his daughter, he understood that God was the only one left to punish.

John had let Asa bury Helen in the churchyard, but the stone wings above her name seemed to him a mark of God's victory. No more kin of his would find their rest there. He was only happy, Helen was only whole and well, on the open ocean. It was land that killed, not sea.

When Tabitha wakes, John cannot go to her for fear. "Will you take something?" he says. "Broth?" She moves her head once, as if to shake it. "Yarborough says you will be climbing trees tomorrow." He stands and then sits again, his head in his hands, his fingers feeling at the roots of his hair. He looks at the grain in the floor of the house that he did not build but occupies.

Tab only sees a shape moving in distress.

"Would you like to sail a bit?" he asks her.

Now she remembers the toy boat wrapped in brown paper, and in that thought is clarity, a small space of focus in the haze.

The second night Tab is sick, John leaves her for an hour in the care of Dr. Yarborough and walks east away from town to Cogdell's plantation, which adjoins Long Ridge, and circles around to the slave quarters behind the rice fields. He knows which is her cabin. A man answers his knock, and calls for Moll. The woman who comes to the door is still young and strong, her hair wrapped tight in a red cloth and her face unscarred. A newborn crawls against her chest. Its hands open and shut, catching folds of fabric, searching for milk.

"What's wrong?" she asks. No matter that he hasn't spoken to her in years, though she once thought of him almost as a brother.

"I'm ashamed to come here like this," he says. His wife died ten years ago, and this woman with the infant had been her property, her maidservant, her confidante, her friend. Though now that he is standing here, he doesn't know whether Moll would have claimed that friendship. "My daughter's sick."

"What is it?"

"They don't know. Yellow fever maybe."

A boy curls around Moll's hip to see the visitor, but she pushes him back into the cabin. "I don't know much about herbs," she says. "And no one here could do much for the fever."

He nods.

She watches him wanting something more. She is sorry for him. She misses Helen, but she has no debt to John or his daughter. After Helen's death, they moved in separate ways; Moll had her own life to battle. She is a field worker, not a guardian angel. His concerns are not greater than hers. The baby begins to cry: a long, piercing syllable that dissolves into hiccups. "We can't do anything for yellow fever," she says again. "Ask some other conjure man."

"I didn't know," he says, gesturing toward the infant. "I should congratulate you."

She waits for him to blush, to back away, to excuse himself, but he doesn't move. He's waiting for something too. If it's sympathy, he knocked on the wrong cabin door.

"And the boy?"

"Davy," she says.

"Can I see him?"

She scratches at her covered hair with her free hand, then calls for her son. The boy runs back to the door, almost bouncing. John is exhausted to see so much frantic energy. He nods once. The boy nods back, three times.

Moll, holding the infant with one loose hand, puts her other palm on Davy's head, runs it along his scalp, squeezing it, as if to feel for soft spots. He shakes his head to free himself, but Moll slips her hand down to his neck to hold him still.

John could stand here and watch this mother love her son for days.

"Where'd you get your coat?" Davy says, pointing a finger toward John's chest.

John looks down and says a tailor in New Bern made it.

"What's his name? In case I wanted one someday."

John waits to see if he's teasing, but the child's eyes are happy and serious, so John gives him the name.

Moll's husband calls out from inside, and she can hear her girls' voices escalating toward a fight. She bounces the baby to calm it, her hand still draped around Davy's shoulders. "I'm sorry I can't help," she says. She should say she'll pray for the child, but she doesn't.

He rubs his face and leaves.

In the morning Tab cannot stand to walk. The dizziness turns her body into vibrating points. John tucks the quilt around her, lifts the damp bundle, and carries her downstairs to rest on the sofa while he gathers meal and potatoes into a sack, some jugs of water. To save her from the graveyard, he must take her to sea. He took her mother once, and being on the water only made her bloom. Tab will get well beyond the reach of Asa's religion. He looks at the paper parcel above the shelves in the hearth room and wonders if a dress could be made of such fine silk aboard a wayward ship, with villains for seamstresses. No, it will be here for their return. She will come back whole and womanly.

Tab's vision is clear this morning, and though her body rejects her guidance, she is well enough to feel a thrill at what the day will bring. She is trailing in her mother's path.

It is Sunday and the ships are come to harbor. Trading ships and whaling ships and ghost ships whose crews know her father. When Mrs. Foushee reads them stories, she calls them buccaneers. Wicked men who lure vessels for the plunder, who tie ladies to the masts and make them scream to call the navies in. John tells her little of those days, so the scenes in Tab's head are of her own devising. She is ten years old, of an age when the wicked are the heroes. She has outgrown tales of moral children.

In the night, when she had called out in pain, John told her they'd set sail with a black crew. She would be the ship's queen, and with her scepter would guide them to the Indies. Sugar, gold, parakeets, beaches without muck and weeds. He told her of the blue and yellow of the islands and the bone-soaking sun and the wild ladies who brewed potions for their lovers. Tab said she didn't have a lover. John told her to hush and keep still.

Now she watches him fumble through the house, shutting windows and picking up oddments, and wishes she could cut a finer figure as the lady of a ship. She senses her face has become unlike herself, for her father won't look at her straight.

When he is ready, he straps the sack across his back and lifts her, still wrapped in the quilt, and with his foot pulls shut the door of their house. He has left a note for Asa, another for his partner in the store. Helen would tell him to stop, he hasn't thought about a hundred things; what about a brush for Tab's hair? If he paused, he would not be able to move again. He has always been led by a buried instinct, and this brought him his wife and it brought him his daughter, so he trusts it now and doesn't go back for a brush for Tab's hair.

He carries her, stopping along the road to adjust the weight, to the harbor, where the only men are foreign and tired eyed; the saints of the town are making their preparations for church. He lays her gently on the ground, leaning up against a hitching post, and searches out his old mate Tom who docks from time to time. In asking for him among the tattered crews, he faces blank looks and evasions. He heads to a man-of-war still loading provisions, and the captain is gracious enough, but he hasn't seen John's friend.

"Do you need extra hands?"

The captain shakes his head.

"I sailed for two years before the war, then put in good service in the army. I could show you letters," he says, though he has no letters.

"I'm sorry," the captain says.

At a smaller schooner, they ask to see his commendations, so he stands tall and tells them with a bite in his eyes that he has worked ships twice as big and for half shares, and they tell him to move on.

He should go back to his daughter, who might be cold, but he can't walk away from the docks. There are no other paths that he can see. A sailor walks past with a load of nets and a familiar beard, and John asks once more about his friend, who would give him passage on any boat.

The sailor pauses and shifts his load. "Tom been strung," he says. "Caught for something, maybe pinching rations." When John doesn't reply, the sailor walks on, dragging rope behind him.

John squints at the south horizon and a flat sea.

"Tom Waldron? He minded mast for me."

John turns to see a young gentleman with a thin patrician nose smoking a pipe, his free hand playing about his ruffled neck.

"Hezekiah Frith," he says, and tilts his head. "Looking for passage?"

"You wouldn't take me. I've a daughter, ill."

"And where are you bound?"

"Merely away. The Indies."

Frith taps his pipe, then tugs his coat sleeves even. "I'm a man short. What ships have you ridden?"

"The *Mohawk*, the *Victory*, the *Tryon*. But a woman —" John says.

"I have no superstitions there. I like them for a cover."

"And the fever."

"We've a physician aboard. Keep her separate and well aired." Frith glances toward the town road and sees the sagging patchwork bundle. "Little girls," he says. "We're making for Bermuda, catching what we will along the way. You'll take Tom's post for no pay. And no pinching. We run small business, and little harm. We'll drop you on the island, and if you sail again, I'll offer shares. Is that a bargain you'll shake to?"

John sees his dead life breathing. He remembers taking another woman on a ship, carrying Helen — not ill, but a bride — on deck, her smile reflected in the sun, the sea not wide enough to mirror their affection. He is here again, grasping, because he is selfish of his child. He cannot lose another piece of his family. But Tab seems to yearn for this too. In his fatherhood, he is protecting her from death and God and misery, and so does what every man would do. He shakes Frith's hand and takes his daughter on board the *Fanny and Betsy*, a cedar-hulled three-mast sloop. From the deck they can hear Beaufort's church bells ringing.

Inside the small church, Asa sits in the last pew. When the service is finished, he will catch Dr. Halling and take him to the white house along the shore to speak words above his granddaughter. John has lost his faith, but Tab is still a green plant growing, absorbent to the Lord. He could not save his daughter, but he will save this little relic of her. There is still time to redeem himself. He bows his head as the visiting priest sermonizes. He should move to a city, where he could hear the gospel weekly. God is always listening, but Asa cannot hear his voice enough.

They stand for a hymn. Soon Tab will be back here beside him, her little hymnal in her hand, her voice ringing out her young faith. They sing verses about heaven and its pleasures, about the narrow sea that separates the living and the dead. Asa's hands begin to tremble. He breathes deeply and hears his chest catch on his exhaling. The voices rise higher.

Another tolling of the bells frees the congregation into a warm October noon. From the steps of the church, they can see down into the harbor, where a single ship is bound for open ocean.

CHAPTER
TWO

The rocking eases Tabitha to sleep, her aching body cocooned in a rope and canvas hammock in a small cabin next to the captain's below the aft deck. She can hear the murmur of her father's voice next door, the sigh of boards above her, the bullying of gulls through the small window cut high in the cabin wall. She presses her ear into the canvas of her bed. Through the fabric, she can hear bells.

Frith sets John to the dog watch, just two hours. In the meantime, the sailor will clean deck with his brethren. John asks the route, and the captain unrolls a map on the table. John stands to the side and looks not at the map but at Frith's face. Frith pulls at the skin below his eyes, digs his thumbs into the flesh behind his ears. He sways. John cannot tell if the captain is still aware of his presence. His eyes do not seem to be moving across the paper but are rather fixed in the depths of the painted ocean.

"We sail straight for the island?" John asks. His voice is too loud.

Frith drops one hand flat on the map, covering the routes, and looks through John. "How old is the girl?"

"Just ten," John says. "Not old enough to tempt your men. You'll tell them." He has been on ships where anything in skirts was a lure. Weeks go by at sea, and morals fade. But surely no man would risk the fever.

Frith nods. "I've one who's five. Fanny."

"The ship's after her, then?"

"The name is not my devising." Frith worries the edge of the map between his fingers. "Rum's the game. We head south first. The hold is too empty yet for going home."

When John returns to the cabin, Tab is sitting in the hammock like a trapped crab, her legs crooked at the knees. She is heaving, retching.

On deck, John leans behind a mop, working at the filth that has grown since yesterday morning. Beaufort harbor had broken up like a reflection and now is gone, the horizon having swallowed his home. They have slipped through the shoals, and now the greenish water has turned dark and gray, the bottom invisibly deep. The men aboard are strangers to him. As a younger man, he had been the darer, the rope swinger, the one who leaned over the rails into the spray. But after ten years on the shore, his hands have grown papery from handling coin and cloth. They turn raw around the wooden handle of the mop.

He has kidnapped his daughter and brought her on a black ship, away from God and medicine, with no hopes but a distant island, the reaching of which will probably require the death of seasoned men. Though the war has ended, these are the men still fighting.

There are no reasons to bring a child on a sloop except selfishness and a wild response to loss. If he had a vision of her as her mother, soaking up the open sea, he has his own willful blindness to blame. Tab is a child; she is sick. He cannot re-create what has already happened. He can imagine Helen as a young woman encouraging this girl's adventure, laughing at John's subterfuge, but as a mother? John never knew her as a mother. She may well have acquired the fierce protectiveness that John is now violating. He has betrayed the woman she would have become.

He wrings out the mop over the side of the ship. He will disembark at Charleston, after the sea air has done its work, and they'll travel back home slowly, by stage, and when she's older, Tab will remember this as something lost and golden, the dreamy heart of a happy childhood. When she is asked how it was to become a woman motherless, she will say, "But I had my father," and will think of seacaps and the swamped roads running between rice fields, the egrets delicately stepping. A slow circle from her home out into water and back through the Carolinas.

Did he board the *Fanny and Betsy* for her, then, to wrest her from a biblical death, a sanctioned passing into God's hungry arms, or had his yearning for landlessness overcome him like a tide? He remembers Asa, after Tabitha's birth, dragging his wife's body away.

The speech of birds fades as her window darkens, and all Tab can hear is the insistent watery press of waves on cedar. She has woken from a nap into the dimming and so cannot place which sill of day she's crossing. The smell of sweat and salted meat reminds her she's not at home, not in anybody's home, but on a barge of plunder. If her knees didn't ache so, she would smile at the thought of it.

A man squeezes in through the door, and, unable to lift or turn in her hammock, she assumes it's her father.

"Ship doctor, miss," and a hairy brown hand reaches into the hammock and fumbles for her wrist. She pulls her arms tight to her side. "Here now," he says, and wrenches an arm out into the open. He holds his fingers on her wrist, and by the candle in his other hand, Tab sees a great round hairy face, bursting with bristles from eyebrow to ear, nose to chin.

"Blackbeard," she whispers. Mrs. Foushee had shown them a picture of the man.

"Yellow fever, they say. Is that what's troubling?" He leans an elbow on the side of the hammock so it rocks outward, nearly tipping her. "Now let me tell you what all I know about the fever. It comes hot and cold, does it, with the welts up your arms and down. Nights, the vapors leave you to go dancing with the devil, I've seen them myself, I have, and in the mornings they come settling back, all wearied out, and that's when the welts turn blue. In ladies the feet take to tapping, and that's the devil's work too, to pound it out of you." He looks at her kindly, at her eyes, which are still staring. "Have your feet been tapping?"

She shakes her head.

"So the cure, you ask me. Most will say bleeding, and that may work, but I'd first give it a good broth to ease the lungs and a little mustard paste to draw the welts back down."

Tab whispers again.

"What's that, my miss?"

"I haven't any welts."

"Oh, that's just time'll do it. Not to worry, your ladyship. Rest up, and I'll be sending the broth in with your father." He lifts his leaning body from her hammock and sends it swaying again. "Cheer up, miss. I've cured half the men I haven't killed."

When John returns to the cabin, his hands blistered and his lower back pinched, Tab is awake and silent in the dark. Below her hammock spreads a small puddle of vomit. He places one hand on her forehead and closes his eyes.

"This is not dying, is it?" she asks.

He pulls away from her, lights a candle, finds an old cloth among the piles of oddments in the cabin, and wipes up the traces of her sickness. "There is no sun you'll not see. How's that for a promise?"

He fetches her broth from the mess table and spoons it from the tin bowl into her mouth, which is a lurid pink.

"What will we see on the islands?" she asks.

John begins again his list of wonders: elephants, he promises, and cinnamon. The landscapes she hasn't seen are the ones that buoy her.

The room is close and warm, lit by the candle that wavers on a shelf. Shadows are larger than objects. A curl of Tab's hair springing free of her sweated face makes a snaking sea monster on the wall. In their quiet, they can hear the clanking of mugs from the mess, the bursts of profane humor, the endless wash of the ocean.

"Did you tell Grandfather?"

John considers. He'd left the letter next to Helen's miniature in the parlor, where Asa would notice it. The older man always sought out the little painting on his visits, holding it when he could. He had a possessiveness in him that encompassed his house, his land, his women. And whatever didn't belong to him belonged to God. Asa would be happy to have the girl in heaven, might consider it safer than Beaufort, but John has no such faith. He could not leave his daughter's body with a man who would not mind it, whose vision of God implied the reclamation of his flock. John believes in flesh. His love survives no transubstantiation.

A seaman has found his fiddle and is setting a simple meter for a few drunken dancers. Soon John is due at his post on the bow, watching the stars again and searching for motion in darkness. Before he'd met Helen, in amongst stints of pirating, he had spent a year on a whaler and learned the smallest undulations of the sea, the telltale kick of spray from idle waves, an underwater hum. Here he must look for nothing but other masts. He leaves Tab's unfinished broth on a shelf and eats his own tack and lime. Her eyes have closed, and he rests his fingers on her cheek once more. Her face has slipped into a fevered sheath. Her shift is damp. The loose curl still stands away from her forehead, trembling in the thin breeze that sneaks in through the cabin window. He kisses her and leaves her, without what the faithful would call hope.

On deck he meets Blue Francis, the ship's surgeon, who asks after his daughter. John thanks him for looking in on her. The doctor smiles and shakes his shaggy head. "If women be the sailors' bane, then I think the young of them be treasures. Little ones are the lights that ease our blackness, a'n't they?"

From the mast, John sees nothing. The waves near the ship are yellow-tipped from the candles burning, the ones farther out are silver. He knows there are bodies beneath him. Below the lip of ocean swim schools of mackerel and drum, below them the whales, dipping to find their feed, and below them all the unnameables, the serpents, the kraken, the giant conger. What he has learned of the Bible are the bits Asa recited to him and the pieces that the sailors tell, the story of Job's Leviathan, who *maketh the sea like a pot of ointment*, who *maketh a path to shine after him; one would think the deep to be hoary*. John sees the monster's frost spread across the water, the unknown of it, the lurking danger universal.

When he was young, John thought the night gave cover to those who would steal him from his bed, who would select him as a prize from the sprawl of cousins he slept among. At night, the shadows pooled and left no inch uncovered. Only when he took to sea did he find the light again, collected as it was in concentrated smears on the sky and water, capping and puncturing the dark. He had taught Tabitha to see this. He had taken her to the marshes in the evenings so she could amend her sight, could watch the sun fade and reconstitute. Now she seems afraid of nothing.

After a burst of laughter from the sailors' bunks, a loud report issues from the stern. The quartermaster is knocking about. These men seem far beyond John's scope. Though once as rowdy and unconcerned as the petty officers, he now finds himself circling around a single set of images — child, God, woman, home — his duty never easing.

The sea air that opens lungs is the same that chafes the skin to scales. There is no version of this play in which he has done right. He has chosen rashly, and the fading stars remind him of the home to which they all will go, whether he professes faith or not. There Helen, if she waits anywhere, is waiting for her daughter.

A loud stirring of sailors and buckets and hauled rope wakes Tab. The sun already washes in through the window over the shelves and barrels and John's empty corner berth. She feels weak, but also hungry. Her muscles that had clenched into resistance have eased again, and she is moved, emotionally, by the desire to stand. In attempting to untangle herself from the tight hold of the hammock, she tumbles to the floor, catching herself with pudding arms. There is no vomit here from the night before. She sits on the planks until her vision clears, then stands like a calf. The ship's rocking is unfamiliar to her feet, and she grasps the rope of her bed to steady herself. There is no mirror in the cabin, but, trading hands on the rope to keep her balance, she takes down her hair and smooths it back into its wrinkled ribbon. Her legs sway. The breaking of the fever has made her giddy. She loses hope for her appearance, but there are none here but unkempt seamen; if she wishes to join their company, a little dirt will not prevent her. She pushes the cabin door open and slides down a short passageway past the captain's room and up three steps into a glory of sunlight and ocean. She is a captive, the slave of notorious buccaneers, the masthead for a ship of villains. Her lungs take in the salt and spray of liberty.

The decks are alive with men and movement, sails snapping and lines pulled and tied, figures climbing masts, the sea bouncing the ship on an endless, landless plane beneath a rounded sky. This is what a proper town should look like, an upturned anthill of activity. She steps into the motion and weaves slowly among the men at their business. Seagulls churn in their wake. Every wave seems to break over a fish's back. Tab is light-headed but certain that she can now do anything with her body. What had kept her father so long from these ragged perfect men? From their house in Beaufort, all they could see was sand and marsh and a still and silent sea. Here, on the *Fanny and Betsy*, even the ocean is a riot.

She balances against the mizzen-mast. Over the crack of the wind-taut sails, the men are singing. She laces her fingers into the rigging. A whistle draws her attention skyward, and she spies a sailor perched on a spar between the main sails and the topsails, his legs dangling like a child's. He waves down at Tab, and she rises on her toes in her enthusiasm to respond.

A seaman wrapping lines by the starboard shrouds calls out, "Johnny, your miss is loose and about!"

Her father comes loping from the bow, swings her by the waist, and sets her three feet from the mast, where, without the wood to clutch, she falters. He grabs her arm to steady her.

"What business have you on your feet, Tab?" John feels her forehead.

"I feel a hundred times improved," she says, and clings to his coat. "Have you seen the ship? Have you been everywhere?"

"I'll carry you back to the cabin and have the doctor look in. You need rest still." John wraps his arm around her back. "It'll be here when you're all well. I'm the one must answer for your health."

Back in the dark cabin, bunched in her hammock, Tab lets Blue Francis poke at her ribs and glance behind her ears. "Seems the welts have whiled themselves away."

"Never *had* welts," Tab says.

"Little ladies don't care for the welts. They leave spots on the face, don't they, and then it's a hard road catching the gentlemen, don't I know. Though I married a lady with the spots and a prettier one would be hard to picture, excepting yourself. Shame to leave her behind, haven't seen her in a dog's year, but I imagine she's fixed things up fine by now and keeps a pot on the fire against my return. In a year or so, whenever we make Barbados again."

Tab struggles to sit up. "Is she a negro, doctor?"

"Can't find any signs on you left, and your little heartbeat is running along smartly. I didn't even have to use the mustard paste, which we don't have aboard anyhow, but could probably purchase in Charleston for such a one as you. Frith'll give me a few pence here and then for oddments. Better captain I've never known, the way he lets us do. I was once a surgeon on a navy ship, full frigate, and men of the queen's own wouldn't give you a bottle of the bark, they wouldn't. They say men under the black flag is nothing but scoundrels, but here I can treat a little miss as right as you please. And now you're fit and fine. Fetch me if aught else should happen, if your toe finds a splinter, or you start seeing merfolk from the decks."

"This is the happiest ship on the ocean, isn't it?" she says.

The doctor squints at her from the lit doorway. "If you call it happy where men die."

She is silent as he leaves.

She has not thought of battles, of raids, of disease, of thirst and starvation. Of cannonballs landing with cracks on the boards of the main deck, lodging with deep thuds in the hull. The sharks waiting to sup on sailors when the ship goes down. She had yellow fever and now is better. Her mother went aboard a ship like this and was a queen. Only the land can kill people. Only the solidness and the long stillness and the heavy quiet can bring them to their knees and press them down until they die for lack of breath. The doctor shouldn't worry about her, but about his land-bound lady, who is likely dying in childbed even as the sun shines on this salt water.

From her bed, she can see only the sky through the small window. A single tern cuts past, crying. She will leave her room again and ask her father about her birthday gift, just after a brief study of sleep. The walk from cabin to mast to cabin has left her legs pleasantly lame. She makes space in her open hands for the toy ship from New Bern, the wooden infant of this grand vessel.

She wakes in the afternoon feeling stronger yet. On deck she searches out the cook and finds him sleeping behind an iron cauldron where a stew is simmering. The smell is rich and just short of rancid. She takes her bowl and biscuit into the sun again and finds a space between two barrels to fold herself, safely distant from the lines. Two dozen men seem to be playing a game with coils of rope, vast sheets of linen, and the open ocean. The sloop is making progress, but Tab cannot tell in what direction they're moving, or whether circles are being transcribed in place of a forward route. Whenever she looks at the sun, it's a step to one side of noon.

Even with the wind, the air is warmer here than on the Beaufort shore. She tucks a bent nail into her dress pocket. Once in Bermuda, she'll find not only shells and crab husks but also the beached carcasses of sea monsters with tusks of ivory. She will help her father build a house there, and everything she does will be an echo of her mother, so John will be content again. This is the life he was meant for, the life Tab had kept him from. Women, with their death, with their birthings, are not fit sailors. But Tab fixes a bargain, neither to die nor to beget life, and she asks the God of her grandfather to witness. Asa had always told her that if she was good, God would be her final home, and though he described it dully, he said her mother was waiting there. Tab is not sure whether she is good, but she knows that in her old home her father was restless, unhappy, wearied. Nothing grew on that shore but Mrs. Foushee and the church, and the ghost of a mother who would always every day be newly dead.

In her corner between the barrels, Tab tells God she will be good, that she will seek adventure and so redeem her mother's absence, and in that moment with the sun on her face like a warm hand, she chooses to believe in his promise of everlasting life. To seal the compact, Tab sings one of Asa's hymns. She sees John by the foremast siphoning powder into small kegs, and though she cannot see him smiling, she knows that he is joyous here, and free.

John labors with new gaiety. His daughter has sprung to life, a fever victim become a child again. He knows that yellow fever always has this pause, this reprieve that leads loved ones to hope, and that afterward the patients are either well or dead. But seeing her body in motion, her legs fumbling across the swaying deck, he swallows hope and lets it burn inside him. He pulled his daughter from the godly quicksand of Beaufort and now, in the clear and open air, he has saved her. He has done for the child what he could not do for the mother. A peace settles on him as he packs the powder kegs and carries them below to the gun deck. This ship is a haven, and even amongst two dozen of the roughest men he has no fear for his daughter. She is less a woman than a thin angel, the specter of her departed mother.

As an unpaid seaman on board a black-flagged sloop with no purpose but idle raids, John has few duties. He scrubs the weather deck, coils lines, sometimes climbs the shrouds to tie the mainsail, though never the topsails, which are another man's province. He tidies the berths below the forecastle deck, where the rest of the sailors sleep, and lends aid to the cook, who has no mate. They apportion the dried meat and barley, the malt and the limes; they ration the rum. John has hardly spoken to Frith since they embarked, though only a thin wall of boards separates their cabins on the quarterdeck.

He takes on some tasks only to keep his hands busy, so that he's not caught dancing with his daughter from foremast to mizzen-mast. After the powder kegs are safe below, he tends to the loose seams between the planks on deck, finding cotton and oakum in the stores and caulking the gaps with fibers and tar. This is a job done sitting down, and requires nothing but pressing hands and a little brush. He should be doing this when the ship is docked and dry and the wood has shrunk, but his fingers need a duty. Here, crouched near the bowsprit, he can look back on the expanse of the *Fanny and Betsy* and observe the small colony of men and the ten-year-old girl, who is sneaking between laboring groups and bending down to catch at what John assumes must be treasure. The sight of her, and her curious hands, brings back John's wife. She was the first to know which objects mattered.

Years ago, he and Helen and the smallest version of Tab were on just such a ship. His wife's belly was growing into a little drum. He asked what sort of mother she would be, and she asked what sort of father, and they laughed, having no guides. The ship was heading north again for home, laden with stolen goods, but that day, in the blue and gold of summer, they were docked at Antigua. The sailors were in town, some spending coins on women, others spending them on trinkets for the women they left behind: carved coconuts, painted bowls, bones. They would sail the next morning, the captain believing that one could out-run the diseases that thrived in the Indies.

In the cabin they shared, not six feet wide and with one hammock hung above the other, the afternoon glowed on the walls. Helen had pulled him here when the men filed off the ship. He asked didn't she want to see Antigua, and she had kissed him, and he said no, he didn't either. This cabin was Helen's refuge when the ship engaged with trade boats on the ocean; even though they were rarely in danger, she was still shy of criminality.

"Come see," she said, her hand tight around his arm.

Her open face reminded him of childhood. There was a song the boys would tease the girls with. "Be kind, my love, be kind," he said, "and you shall ever find —"

"That a long, long absence can't alter my mind." She smiled.

They both were children once; and here she was, with child.

She made him sit cross-legged on the floor. Her dark hair had glints of bronze. She took a box with a metal clasp from the shelf and sat before him, the bare soles of her feet pressed together, her stomach a little ball beneath her skirts. He reached to touch her.

She held up her hand. "I wanted to show you," she said.

Helen pulled from the box a series of strange objects — strange not because they were uncommon but because they had found their way into a box, gathered by a single hand. She first held out the button, taken from his coat when she was mending it, and then the glass rubbed smooth from Grenada. A musket ball. Three inches of frayed rope from when the lines were trimmed. He laughed at the pit of a plum.

"You kissed me with the fruit still in your mouth," she said. He had not remembered.

These were her treasures, the bits of life she collected to remind herself of life, the tokens of experience. Her story of land and sea. He had wondered what she needed them for, what eventuality she was predicting.

She lined them up on the wooden floor, in order of size. He held his arms open, and she crawled into him, the two — or three — of them in a tight knot. He kissed her ears and said there was no need for memory, that's how much he loved her. She tucked her head into his neck.

A sailor stopped by with fresh baked fish from shore, and they squeezed into one hammock and ate the fish with their fingers, and he put his head on her stomach and listened, and she watched the row of treasures march from the brass bell down to the tiny broken pearl, and the light slipped down the window and faded into the ocean, and the boisterous noise of men on land accompanied their sleep.

He is careful now not to forget things.

He tamps another line of oakum into a seam. This world is blue and brown and white. The sky and water with their indeterminate shades of paleness and depth reflect only each other. This is the purity that existed for him and Helen, and here it is again, just waiting to be taken up.

At dusk, he finds Tabitha spidered onto the web of ratlines and pries her off, a laughing bundle. They gather with the others at the mess table and John helps the cook serve another stew and heels of bread. When the meal is doled out, he sits Tab down and with his body shields her from most of the men's wildness. Other than the ship surgeon, they've developed no particular fondness for the girl and find her little different from an indentured boy too young for whiskers, and of even less use. Their language is not tempered in her presence.

Blue Francis bangs his mug on the table twice. "If it's ghosts you're after," he says in a hoarse voice, and the others roll their eyes and blow through their lips, adjusting themselves for a long tale, bound to be false. "Listen, listen," he says. The curve of his back rises higher than his shoulders, and he leans into the table with his arms spread out on the grease-spotted wood.

John interrupts him. "Nothing bloody, Frank. You forget the young ones." He keeps one hand on his daughter's back while he sops up the rest of his stew.

The doctor winks at Tab and turns back to his audience. "It were on the *Bonny Jane* some score years ago, in the —"

"When you were just an old man," someone calls out.

"That's right, just me and your wench," he says.

John tries to nudge Tab out of her seat, but she begs to stay.

"It were a slaving ship and we were nearing Charleston for the trade with more than half the bodies still well and good."

"The others?" Tab whispers, and John tosses his head to one side to signal "overboard."

"They made their moanings, of course, so the whole ship sounded like a bull with its neck cut, but we'd been used to such for weeks and paid it no mind. The last night before port, Captain sent Little Tom up the topgallant to watch for lights and Little Tom quivering in his boots, just as shivered as a boy can get. Had never seen a black before and thought they were singing for his soul." Blue Francis peers over at Tab, whose head cranes out from behind John. "Just about your age, miss. Now Tom was used to ghosts, for wasn't a ship didn't have a dead sailor wandering around it, his neck cracked from falling from sail to spar, or his hair all floating up from the water drowned him. So when I heard him start the screeching and saw him clambering down the yards like a man chased, I thought he'd seen something solid. He ran straight for the captain's cabin, saying it's raining blacks, his hands swatting all about his head. I looked up and don't see nothing, so I followed him, shouting that there weren't any such things, but he's shrieking and batting his hands around and now the rest of the men woke up and come out to see. Little Tom busts through the captain's door, and the devil damn me if the captain didn't rise up from his bed with his pistol in hand and shoot him clean through." He pauses for effect. Some of the sailors pick at their teeth. "I held his head in my hands as his life slipped out of him and he said, 'Blue Francis, they was blacks raining down on me, they was falling from heaven right on me, clawing and moaning and calling my name,' and before I could tell him they was just ghosts, he dropped his head down and died right there."

"So the negroes go to heaven and the rest of us damned to hell?" a seaman calls out, and there is a clanking of tin mugs and bowls. As Tab twines her arms around her father's chest to stop her own heart from beating fast, one man begins a beat on the table while two more stand and stomp about. The company sings words Tab's never heard, and John carries her back to their berth, across the new-caulked deck, under the white stars.

Held in her hammock again, Tab asks her father why some bodies would go to heaven and others to hell. She knows of these places from Asa, but why would sailors be damned instead of slaves, and why were haints always wicked?

"It was just a story," he says.

"Ghosts aren't true, are they?"

John smooths her hair back, which is growing knotted without its brush. "When folk die, it's just their bodies. There's something inside that stays alive always."

"Our souls," Tab says.

"Souls, spirits, ghosts. Memories. I always remember your mother."

"And she's in heaven, don't you think?"

"Some call it that," John says. "She's wherever there's goodness, I imagine."

Tab closes her eyes and speaks in a whisper. "I don't see her." When John takes his hand away, she tries to make the miniature come to life, her mother's small head with green points for eyes, a ribbon round her neck. She moves the head around her mind, placing it in different rooms, on the shore, on deck. It never moves, or smiles.

"You're what's left of her," John says, and she opens her eyes. "If you wonder where she is. I sometimes think she's all in you."

54

"Do pirates always sing such bad songs?"

He laughs. "No."

Tab catches his hand between hers and smiles up at her father. He leans down and kisses her forehead, which is cool and dry, and he hums quietly as she lets her muscles ease into sleep.

In the morning, Tab wakes in a writhing green room. The cabin is trembling. No, her eyes are trembling. She sits and fills her lap with bile, then crawls out of the hammock and lands in a heap on the floor. Her nose is wet and she wipes it against the boards, leaving a trail of red. Something is running fast in her chest. Her heart runs so fast it leaves a cool breeze fluttering through her limbs. There is no heaviness left in her body, only a froth of pain. Through the window, she sees a rain of black bodies, mouths open, her mother pale among them.

She starts to shake and is turned inside out. What existed within her, secret, unseen, is flung on the floor, her vomit, her blood, her limbs spasming away from the core of her. She is an oak leaf spinning in the moat, moss blown by her own breath. Her very particles are leaving her. The room falls into shadow. Her delirium can no longer coalesce to find her mother's ghost in this mirage. The gull calls splinter around her head. The world is breaking.

John returns to the cabin with two red potatoes in his hand and finds his daughter in convulsions on the floor. He falls onto Tab's body, pressing his weight into her to stop her shuddering. A passing sailor looks in, runs for the doctor. The potatoes roll to the corner of the room, then roll back as the sloop crests a swell. Her body is beginning to quiet when Blue Francis hurries in. John looks up, his arms still around his daughter, and shakes his head. The doctor gently lifts John away, rolls the girl onto her side to clear her mouth and free her tongue, and kneads her arms and legs until she is quiet. He tells John to fetch water, and the father stumbles onto the open deck. The tears dry and shrink on his face. There is no emotion the wind cannot erase.

He wraps his arms through the knotted shrouds holding up the mast and hangs there, rubbing his forehead against the rope. This day was always coming. Since losing Helen ten years ago, his life has been a series of breaths held. He only lives to wait for loss. Without believing in the God of salvation and forgiveness, he has faith in God the Punisher.

When he returns, the doctor is cutting thin lines in his daughter's arm, drawing blood in beads to the surface. He looks at John as his fingers wrap around Tab's elbow. Her face is yellow now, her jaundiced skin standing out from the white of her shift. Her eyelids flutter but do not open. Her mouth parts and closes like a fish. John presses his ear to her chest and hears the sound of a woman walking through an overgrown garden, her silk dress brushing against, caught, torn by rose bushes. Tab's heart is walking in that garden.

The doctor digs his fingers into his beard and loosens the tangles. "I wish we had some balsam, to spread a little on the skin, but it would be more for

56

easing than the cure. We have a man was in Philadelphia some weeks ago, and many was laid up with it, no one knowing how to do. Nothing left but to give the bark and cool her down a bit. Any humors in her will leave through the bleeding once they catch a smell of salt air."

John points to the drops of blood along Tab's arms. "That's not enough, is it?"

"She's just a little one, a'n't she, sir? Look at the body of her."

"Bleed her more," John says.

"She's as thin as poles and the heart's not beating strong."

John grabs the lancet from the doctor's hand and cuts into his daughter's yellowing forearm; a small stream of blood flows onto the linen of her dress.

At the stab, the girl wakes, her face twisted. Unable to cry, she leans to the side and heaves up the contents of her stomach, which are black and wet. Her eyes do not open.

"The black bile, sir," the doctor says, as if it were a sign John could read. He watches the surgeon clean up Tab's messes, the black vomit off the floorboards, the blood off her yellow arms.

When she is smooth and clean again, the doctor brings in a blanket wrung in cold water to lay over her body. "I gave the word to Captain, sir," he says. "He let you off watch." He lingers in the door. "I can't do for her more than any other man, but no less either. I never did have a lady patient. She's a lamb in God's hands now, just a child who might be going home."

* * *

Through the afternoon, John and Tabitha wake and sleep, one crying out from dreams, the other wrenching in pain. John finds one of the potatoes and eats it raw. When she groans, he pulls himself up and rests his hands on her cheeks, absorbing the heat. When she shivers, he pushes the wet blanket off and lets it fall with a slap to the floor.

The room darkens and John lights two candles. He eats the salted pork a sailor brings him, but Tab consumes nothing. Even the water he pours into her mouth dribbles out. In ten more years, she would look just like her mother. The candlelight catches the blood that is beginning to seep from her eyes and nose. Her lips are already tinged with red.

Her form — bleeding, limp, and pale — resembles the crucifix hanging in Asa's parlor. He used to sit and stare at Christ's body sagging on the wall while he waited for Helen's company. Helen herself had died with none of the weakness of self-sacrifice. Her cheeks had been flushed, her arms plump, her eyes bright with exertion. She had borne Tabitha in a tumult of sound and motion; only when the baby was followed by the pooling of blood did she turn white, but she slipped away still vibrant, surrounded by the pulsings of life. In the vigor of her death, John could deny God's power. It seemed her own doing.

But this is different. Tab's life is leaking away, is being siphoned. What force is sucking at her but the universe? What power but a black and holy one?

When the dusk has become night and only one side of things is lit by the candle glow, Tab murmurs, "The ship."

He stirs from a half rest and twines his fingers in hers. She glances down at her open palm. "We *are* on a ship," he says. "The *Fanny and Betsy*, bound for Bermuda. You're in the cabin now."

"Small," she says, and gestures with her empty hand. "Birthday."

"You had a birthday a few days ago. Turned ten years old. You were ill, so I brought you on the ship for a little sea air."

"Birthday," she repeats. A tear mingles with the blood from her eye and leaves a pink streak across her temple.

"I'm sorry you weren't well for it. I had a present for you."

She squeezes his fingers.

"I left it in Beaufort — it was too fine for pirates. It will be there when we return. But I'll tell you what it was. Five yards of finest silk, to make a grand dress for you, a lady now." Tab closes her eyes. "Blue it is, with vines going up and around in pink and green. I'll ask Mrs. Randolph to make it into something for parties and such, and you'll be the little queen. The image of your mother."

Tab is weeping now.

"You'll be well in a few days, and I'll order Frith to turn us around and take us to port whenever you please."

"The little ship," she says, and closes her hand.

In this last hour of consciousness, Tab floats on the ocean, no ship beneath her, surrounded by her mother and father and grandfather and any brothers and sisters who were caught unborn in her mother's womb. She might have had four siblings by now, all of whom would follow her to the shore and curl up next to her at night to keep her warm in the winters. She is part of a family halted. She blames the sea for being romantic and God for killing. The room fills up with ghosts.

Her grandfather is singing death to her. She asks her hands to cover her ears, but they do nothing. She will not yield. Her limbs are steeled against God's assault.

Her hairs enter each pore with pinpricks; her whole body is alive to the sharpness of pain. The candlelight in the room blends with the darkness, and her vision slowly vanishes in a blackening muddle. The voices rise around her. Her hammock is wet with sweat and blood, is wet with the sea. She is leaving the world in a red storm, through the body of one already dead. She can now remember what it was like to be born.

The ship is quiet at night. The birds have found their rest somewhere in this wide emptiness, and the sailors are asleep. The wind has slipped out of the sails. The ocean holds them gently.

John wipes the blood from her face. A spark still lingers beneath her skin. A soul preparing for a journey, if he believed in such. Nothing Asa said to him he ever understood, yet now he tries to cull the verses and hymns that spoke of immortality. He cannot let go.

What succor he found after Helen's death existed in this girl, and with her spirit blown away like a dandelion puff, there will be nothing but a vastness unfillable. The holes will swallow him. He holds tightly to her yellowed arm. He does not realize he is praying.

He wakes in the morning with a chill, his body sprawled across hers. He moves as if to close the window in his bedroom, but the rolling of the ship reminds him. The coldness comes from his child's form. In her hammock she is held as sweetly as in a coffin. The jaundice still blooms on her skin. He lays her hands upon her chest in a cross and kisses her forehead, which feels like stone on a fall morning. It is time to take her home.

He finds Frith on the bridge deck. Blue Francis is there, looking sorrowful, to take over the wheel for his captain.

"We're still a day out of Charleston," Frith says. The two men face the stern and the slow boil their passage causes in the water. "We don't keep the dead."

"I'll build her a box," John says.

"And bury her where?"

"There's a space next to my wife."

"She'll rot before she arrives, even in October. There's no dishonor in the sea. We've a man can serve as priest, if that's what you're after."

His fingers are still tinged red with her blood. "It must be done right this time," John says.

"I'm not the master of your conscience," the captain says. "I've a ship to keep. I'll drop you off at port, for you're little use, and you'll take the child with you if you must hold to her. But it's a long road back to Beaufort, and there's no stopping the smell of her." Frith places a hand on John's back as brief as a lighting fly.

"Condolences," he says. He steps among the lines and begins giving orders for the day.

Blue Francis turns and whispers to John. "You want to get her safe home?"

John glances at him, his hand still rubbing the stern rail.

"My grandmother had to mind a body once, back when she and my aunt, just young enough to walk, were taken by Indians. They scalped Aunty in no time, they did, and said my grandmother was plenty welcome to stay and find herself a family and pass the corn, but there was my grandmother wailing for the loss. The Indians being plenty obliging gave her a pot to pickle her in. With the last of the British coins she had on her, she bought drink off the Indians and filled the pot high and kept the little miss, my aunty, for three years before her husband's brother found where she was hiding and carried her and the pot off too, and they married, paying no mind at all to my grandfather, and lived happy and had my mother and all the rest." Blue Francis turns back to the listing wheel. "Rum's kept below."

John sleeps on the floor below his daughter in the hammock, on the boards stained with her illness. The soaked blanket brought to cool her is still in a wet heap

62

in the corner. In this new life in which nothing is left to him, he is hounded by God. This god is a storm that requires settling, and he cannot think of what would calm it other than relinquishing Tabitha, consecrating his daughter in God's name. Peace has eluded him since he watched Helen's body taken away by his father-in-law without his consent, and there is nothing for it now but to believe in his own insignificance, to cast his lot to the gale and let his body be washed over, purified. His sin was in clinging to his wife and daughter as his own. But they are gone, and that is done. He lets go of the sail, watches it fly into the storm's wind.

In the evening when the men are at mess, John takes a bucket below decks to the storeroom, where he tilts the kegs until he finds the ones that slosh. He uncorks a barrel and empties the rum a bucket at a time, taking the excess above to throw overboard, until the barrel is half full. With his knife he carves the lid off and stares down into the liquid left. He walks quietly back to his cabin and peels Tabitha out of her hammock, hoisting her thin body over his shoulder and wrapping his arms around her legs, which are brushed with the soft fur of youth. Her feet are bare. They must have been cold at night.

Through a burst of laughter from the foredeck, he carries her down to the storeroom and props her against the open barrel, his hands under her arms keeping her from sliding. John shifts his gaze from his child to the keg. He lays her on the floorboards, folds her knees to her chest, and wraps her dead arms around them. He lifts and lowers her pinioned body into the rum — feet first, then squeezing the center of her tight, then the rest of her, watching the alcohol float up around her. Her hair is caught by the rising liquid and it fans out, gold on gold.

His daughter.

He nails the lid of the barrel shut and reseals the wood with oakum and tar. With chalk he draws an X upon the side and below it the year: 1793. There is no reason to mark time except to ask God to slow his ravages.

Above decks he takes his plate of meat and bread and accepts the stares of the seamen, who know he carried the fever onto their ship. John takes Blue Francis aside and tells him of the barrel the doctor must roll off the ship in Charleston, straight into the market to sell, and there to deliver into John's hands.

"And when Captain asks for the money of it?"

"You've lost it. It's stolen."

"Well, it's not my rum," Blue Francis says. "I'll tell him Cook asked for a few extra dollars for salt and flour so we needs sell a keg. He doesn't keep accounts. But I wished you'd have let me have the extra."

A day later in Charleston, a bristle-bearded sailor rolls a barrel, lighter than its kin, off the *Fanny and Betsy* while his mates search out the taverns. He barters with a few merchants in the dock markets and then slips into an alley alongside a churchyard, where he passes his burden to a taller man, still young in the face. The second man hires a cart and horse with what's left of his purse and hoists and secures the barrel with the aid of the hostler. It's a warm day for October, and both men sweat. The hostler thinks he'll be offered a pull from the keg, but the man drives off in silence. In five or six days, he will reach Beaufort, where he will make a hole beside his wife to lay the cask of his daughter. There he will wait to see how God scripts the rest.

Part Two

1771–1782

CHAPTER
THREE

For her tenth birthday, she is given a girl named Moll, who stands in the corner with blue ribbons in her hair. After her father leaves them, Helen stares at the child and wishes she had been given the ribbons instead. Helen had asked her father for a silver brush with boar bristles and a hand mirror. She has no sense of what to do with a negro girl other than to make her fetch things. She advances slowly, and when the girl doesn't flinch, Helen reaches out and unties the satin loops.

"Those mine," Moll says.

Helen winds them between her fingers. "I'll tell my daddy."

Moll throws out an arm, grabbing at Helen, who twists around to protect her plunder. Moll scrambles onto the other girl's back, and within moments of the bedroom door closing, the two are scuffling on the ground, pulling at each other's ears. Their struggle is silent, governed by the prideful solidarity of childhood. Moll, taller by an inch, prevails, and the girls lie on the floor breathing heavily while the slave twines the satin ribbons around the short puffs of her hair.

"You try again, I'll kill you," she says.

At dinner, Helen makes a point of being sullen. Her father hands her the knife to cut the cinnamon cake Mrs. Randolph baked, saying, "You're the lady of the house now," and Helen folds her arms across her chest. Moll stands again in the corner, in the shadowy space between the falling light from two windows, her ribbons glinting. After Asa has served Helen a slice of cake with a sigh, she glares at the slave, stuffing her mouth in revenge.

The girls sleep in the same room that night, one on a mattress stuffed with goose feathers, the other on the floor. When Helen wakes in tears, Moll climbs into the bed and lets the smaller girl curl up against her shoulder. Even in September, the floor gets cold without sun.

In the morning, Helen drags Moll to the neighboring plantation owned by Mr. Cogdell, to the cabin that has been set aside for meetings and church. A handful of older slaves gathers on the first few benches, their hands in their laps. Helen stands before them.

"This is Moll, and she was given me for my birthday yesterday, which makes me ten. She's a teacher too. Any questions, you may ask her."

"Who's her people?"

Helen looks at the gray-haired woman on the front row and turns to Moll, who shakes her head. "She hasn't any but me," Helen says. "It may be she comes from Virginia." She leads the group first in the alphabet, and then in catechism. Moll stumbles along with her, mimicking her authority. No one asks her any questions.

After her lesson is done, Helen takes Moll back to her father's land and down to the river that elbows in from the sound and still carries a salt taste. Helen is a poor swimmer, but she is hot and feels a certain responsibility as a host to show Moll the charms of Long Ridge. The girls strip down to their shifts and float.

"Next time, you may lead them in ABCs," Helen says. Above her are only a few thin streaks of clouds.

"I should, I'm older."

Helen lifts her head from the water. "How much?"

"Eleven. You wasn't even born when I was."

"And you know your catechism?"

"I know more than that."

Helen tries to tread water, keeping an eye on Moll to make sure she doesn't do any tricks. She once had a friend who did somersaults in the water and always splashed her. "Most folks are slow," she says, "so that's about all we can teach them before their heads are full. First business is God, since that's who'll watch over them."

"He watches over black folks?"

"Black and white both," Helen says. "And heathen Indians. Everyone who believes in him goes to heaven."

"And them who don't believe?"

"They will. That's our duty, Moll. We are handmaids of the Lord."

"That like slaves?"

Helen lets her feet drift down to feel in the weedy muck, and stands. She lowers her head so only her nose breaks the surface of the water, her loose hair hanging in strands around her face. She looks at the dark reflection of her own eyes. "I suppose," she says, and with her hands pushes a ripple of waves toward Moll.

"Don't you get it in my ear." Moll paddles away from Helen, keeping her head above water like a muskrat.

"Watch out for the big hole over there," Helen says. "Snapping turtles live in it, so don't put your feet down."

Moll paddles quickly back. "You're lying."

"This creek is mine, and you don't know anything about it."

"That's enough of that, then," Moll says, heading for the bank.

"Wait!"

The girls watch each other. Moll makes a noise of exasperation and dives beneath the surface. She comes up a few seconds later with a shell in her hand. "Didn't see any snappers," she says. She scoops water with the shell and pours it on her other hand. This is to show that she is not afraid.

Helen smiles and dips down so the creek brushes her chin. "It's almost like you being baptized. Here, what's your name?"

"Don't be foolish."

Helen claps her hands on top of the water, sending up a plume of spray. "What's your *name?*"

"Moll!"

"And who gave you this name?"

"Some white man."

"No, you say, 'My godfathers and godmothers in my baptism.' "

"Don't have no godfathers." Moll drags herself onto the river bank, her pale shift turning brown from the silt. Her hair is wilting.

"Well, it's what you say. If you want to teach it to the others, you need to learn. Here, I'll be your godmother, and I'll name you Moll."

The girl on the bank throws her shell at the girl in the water. Helen recites the next few questions, then races herself to a half-sunken log, where a sprig of oak leaves is still growing green.

It is 1771, and Long Ridge sits on the edge of the sound, siphoning the water for its mill, and pushes back through marsh and bottomland into flatwoods, where pines are tapped for turpentine. The house was built to be temporary, but in the years since its hasty construction by his forebears, Asa has added two wings, a classical facade, and a brood of outbuildings. A staircase sweeps ten feet above the root cellar to a shaded porch and a wide white door that faces the sea. Narrow steps behind the house lead from the servants' pantry to what Asa calls the acres, where the smaller pines and scrub trees have been cleared to create pathways among the towering longleaf. This is where boys would have played, if he had had sons.

Asa was born on this land, when the house stood on four posts and was just rough boards pegged together and covered bit by bit, when his father had time, in cypress shingles. His family logged and built ships and began the project of acquisition that Asa would inherit. Turpentine was the business of the future. It required only a few bound slaves of his own and the rest hired, so it allowed Asa to join the ranks of coastal planters without their fear of black hands slashing white throats in sleep. His wife had been a neighbor, and he was more pleased when he stretched his log fence around her lands than when he first felt her warmth in their marriage bed. He never loved her as he should've till she was gone. But both acres and woman contributed to a singular image that Asa continues to pursue.

Weekdays he sends his daughter to pretty Miss Kingston, who teaches her letters and ciphering. Helen brings these skills back to Long Ridge to practice on the slaves. She is also learning the harpsichord, which shows off the length of her neck. Her education will be a stamp of status, and Asa sees enough of the old world in the new to recognize that the appearance of wealth can be as valuable as wealth itself. In her exuberance and opinion Helen is nothing like her mother, who was exactly the sort to be married well and loved calmly. Perhaps she would have taught her some of this passivity. But Helen's only mothers have been substitutes: the teacher, the cook, the slave. If she can't have a woman to hold her and love her, she should have a woman to order around. Moll, at least, will give her the pride and responsibility of stewardship. His daughter must be tamed enough to bring a husband and heir to the land, but otherwise her whims are of little concern to him.

Helen gets the chicken pox a few days before Christmas. When her skin turns rosy, Asa is at the meeting house in town, discussing taxes with the elders. The colonial delegate from Beaufort has recently died, his body lost in a shipwreck and nothing for his wife to bury, and the elders ask Asa, as the next wealthiest landholder, to take his place in a room in New Bern and uphold their interests. Asa is in the business of empire building, though his vision is narrow. He is training his daughter to one day raise his grandson well, to be an image the grandson will recall, as a man, with satisfaction. He has no doubts that there will be a grandson. He accepts the elders' offer.

Home again, he finds his daughter ablaze with fever on the sofa, idly stretching her arms out while Moll dances close and spins away, just shy of being caught.

"What is this?" he asks, reaching a hand toward her forehead but pulling it back again before touching her.

"Moll says conjure," Helen says. Moll is now straight and still by the fireplace, head down.

"We'll send for Stevens." He looks around for a blanket to put over his daughter. "Mrs. Randolph?"

"She's washing," Helen says.

Mrs. Randolph has a family of her own, all yellow haired, behind the fields where the townspeople grow their rice. She rolls her sleeves up past her elbows when she works, and when she is sitting with her skirts bunched, bent over some pot or board, Asa has seen her calves above the limp collapse of her stockings. She is only a woman to keep Helen fed and scrubbed, not a replacement for his wife.

He finds her behind the house, kneeling over a soapy bucket in the small garden that is decaying in winter, her hands thrashing a pair of breeches in the water. *His* breeches. She describes the measures she's taken — some brandy and a little willow bark — and says she's had children with just the like and they're all alive yet. "Except for Betsy, and little Andrew, but they hadn't chicken pox, sir."

Asa twists his hands behind his back and nods. "I'll send Moll for Stevens." There is no sense in having so many women on his property.

Mrs. Randolph smiles at him again in that simple, maternal way that stings him. He leaves her, her wet arms red with the chafing cold.

When Stevens arrives in the evening, Moll, tired from her jog to town, is curled on the parlor floor, her head resting on Helen's blanketed legs. Both girls are asleep. The two men consult in whispers by the fire, which sends coughing sparks into the room. The doctor shakes his head to reassure; little danger here. He prescribes rest and alternating heat and cold to confuse the illness and any devils responsible. Asa presses his hand and sees him down the front stairs, at the base of which Stevens's horse is stamping.

He carries Helen upstairs to the room she shares with the slave. She is quiet and not unhappy. She lets her hand linger on Asa's arm after he rests her in the bed. A doll made of dried rushes with a braided waist lies on the pillow next to her. It fits in Asa's palm.

"Moll made it," Helen says.

"For you?"

"She lets me play with it sometimes. You can leave it on the dressing table."

These are the relationships that should be managed by women; mothers are the ones who prevent slaves from slipping out of place. He fears that he has somehow allowed an unraveling.

In the morning, Helen's redness has mellowed some, and she is well enough to be carried downstairs again, where she and Moll play rummy by the window. Helen leans her cheek against the glass to feel the air outside.

"What is it you'd like for Christmas?"

Moll thinks, fingering her cards. She brings them up to her mouth and nibbles at the edges.

"Stop!" Helen slaps a hand out.

Moll pulls her cards down again. "I do have dreams about a yellow dress."

"You're being vain."

"You got one," Moll says.

"And I've a right to it."

Moll sets down her cards and crosses her arms. "You'll give me what you'll give me. No use in me wishing."

"What about a little Bible of your own?" Helen asks.

"And you read it to me?"

"You know most of the letters on your own now. Come, it's been your turn for ages." Helen fans herself while Moll sifts through her cards again, slowly selecting a knave, which Helen snatches the moment it's laid on the table.

Disease has left Long Ridge by Christmas, and Helen is pleased with her complexion. The few slaves gather by the back steps and call *Christmas gift*, and

Helen takes them bundles of fabric and oranges. One older man spits into a clump of weeds.

Inside, Helen unwraps a wool coat and a novel from her father and an apron from Mrs. Randolph, who has stitched the girl's name in pink thread, copying out the letters from Helen's own lesson book. Later, when Mrs. Randolph and Moll are exchanging gifts in the pantry, she tells her father that she doesn't read novels.

"This one was said to be very moral. The author tells about his travels, which I thought you would enjoy."

"I read the first page and it seems silly," Helen says. She is ten years old, not a child.

"You'll be the judge. Surely a diet of prayer alone —"

"Prayer *alone*, Papa? There is nothing better; that's what Miss Kingston says. If I'm to save myself and all the negroes, I must keep on the straight path." She offers him the novel on outstretched hands, as if she were holding a dead toad. "You'd do well to heed the Lord's call yourself."

"The Lord doesn't speak to me, child."

"The day will come when the deaf shall hear the words of the book. Isaiah."

Asa wonders if he should remove his daughter from Miss Kingston's care.

In her room, Helen folds her new coat into the armoire, next to her dead mother's gilt-edged Bible, which she hides under her stays so Moll won't steal it. She likes to think of her mother's slender fingers turning through the gospels, or maybe her fingers were stout, but surely they left a trace on the pages. Miss Kingston is not actually so religious, but she told the girls once that God was a woman's province, and this made sense to Helen. Women were the ones who died.

Mrs. Randolph smoked the ham, but Helen brings it to the table, where she and her father eat alone.

In the afternoon, Helen leads a service in the cabin and a few slaves attend, sucking their oranges. She has arranged some green pine boughs and strands of ivy along the small table that serves as an altar. She emphasizes the importance of being kind because Jesus was, and when she mentions that it's his birthday, a few of the congregants are surprised. She leads them in a carol, which she sings partially in Latin to impress her audience. They mumble along. Her fervor is surely contagious. When the slaves can no longer keep the fire, they leave, and Helen counts it a good day. Souls are always ripe for saving.

In the evening Moll dresses her in green silk for a neighbor's Christmas ball, where she is always the youngest one invited. The other girls her age wear plain white and have no hand in plantation management. They have two parents kissing them to sleep at night, long before Helen is in bed.

Moll asks if she can come, and Helen slaps her on the bottom. In the ensuing chase, a silk sleeve is torn, and Mrs. Randolph sews it up by candlelight before the carriage comes. Moll eats an iced cookie and under the table kicks Helen, whose arm is pinned to inaction by Mrs. Randolph's needle.

Miss Kingston is at the ball in taffeta, and the teacher and student dance together, pausing for breath beneath a mistletoe. The woman, blushing, kisses Helen on the forehead.

That night, curled together like cats, Helen tells Moll that when she's a lady, there won't be room for a slave in her bed. Miss Kingston is dancing through her head, the ghost of her mother behind her, keeping time.

"When'll that be?" Moll asks. Her eyes are closed and she has already drifted in and out of a dream.

"Very soon, I should think."

In 1778, Helen is sixteen. Asa now spends weeks at a time in New Bern, waiting for the British, too awkward to wield a musket, too proud to hide at home. His involvement in the Provincial Congresses doomed him to patriotism, though his inclinations are entirely loyalist. The turpentine business is prospering with his daughter looking after the books; she has inherited his interest in precision. In the airy hall of government, he half-listens to the arguments for new levies and fixes his gaze beyond the windows overlooking a grove of blooming dogwood. Asa imagines a governorship, if these efforts on the part of young men are not in vain, or some permanent post that caters to his penchant for organization and control. Perhaps he will lay roads from Wilmington to the back woods, from the coast to the Cherokees' rocky outcrops.

Arrangements for Helen must be made soon. When the younger delegates propose further military engagements, Asa recommends simplicity and speed. The war interrupts stability. In Beaufort alone, most of the marriageable men are absent. The town is becoming a macrocosm of Long Ridge. When he returns home during recesses, he seems to trespass on a woman's world. The solution for his daughter's slave is more straightforward: Cogdell, his rice-growing neighbor, has a young man, skilled, who requires some discipline. The man had been corrected once after an incipient plot but was not counted dangerous enough to outweigh his usefulness in smithing. There is nothing to settle a man like a woman. A match will also fetter Moll, who because of Helen's sporadic indulgences is becoming willful.

He closes his eyes against the filtering sun. As he ages, he finds his body resting more, and his mind taking longer walks. Here he usually finds his wife again. Shapeless, still, silent. Her chaos muted. The strongest image he has of her is the last. He was kept from the birthing room, or rather, he kept himself, and spent the afternoon picking apples from the back garden so the wind wouldn't toss them against the house. The sky was low and gray and the birds had mostly vanished. A butterfly still fluttered in the banks of sage, its orange lighting the dimness. He could hear waves crashing into the marsh. The slaves had disappeared from the pine groves. In the absence of their chatter and the crying of seabirds, Asa caught the first high whine of his daughter, the first of his children to live past infancy and the last to be born. They had been married four years, and two children had come and slipped away before he felt like a father. The torrents of rain hit, and by the time Asa was blown back inside, the apples rolling from their basket, his wife was already gone. Her soul had taken cover with the thrushes and the gulls, had found a dark corner squeezed between slaves, had walked into the protective darkness and let the wind carry her away. An elm cracked on the east lawn and tumbled onto the house, its crown scraping across their roof. The midwife and the doctor jostled for the child and brought her out screaming. The mother remained, limp and damp, her body to be redeemed when the storm had passed.

Not Asa, but a slave had done it, had fetched his mistress's body and carried her, shawled and still wet, to the surgeon, whose son built coffins out of pine.

Death is not unusual. He had lost three brothers, two newborn sons before Helen's birth. His parents long dead, his wife in the ground with other men's wives. This war would claim thousands more. Bodies are weak, just flesh and bowels. Men should be surprised that they live at all. Asa opens his eyes, content. The Assembly has decided to ask the women for homespun cloth, and Asa concurs. The dogwood blossoms lift on a breeze.

Helen is crouched behind the altar in Cogdell's cabin, her hands clutching the table legs for support. Moses, who is twenty years old and crosshatched with scars and muscle, throws his Bible at the wall above her head. The book falls to the floor, pages exposed, like a shot bird. She shuts her eyes and says she will have him beaten for disobedience. When she opens them, he is gone. She has been instructing him in Christian behavior since she was a child.

82

Safe on her own land again, she finds Moll, who is spending Sunday by the sound, her feet plunged in briny muck. A boiled egg is half in her hand, half in her mouth. Spring has brought with it the ripe smells of decay, uncovered by melting frost. In another month, Long Ridge will begin to smell brighter, green and new. Helen removes her shoes and stockings with shaking hands and wades into the cold water. She carries her skirts to keep them dry.

"I told him of Father's orders."

"You can say all you like, no one's marrying no one," Moll says.

"It's not his choice."

"He told you about the girl he already has? Full up with child?"

"I'm the manager while Father's away." The spring-sluggish fish are beginning to kiss her ankles.

Moll throws the yolk into the river and sucks her fingers. "I don't see anyone hitching *you* to a stranger."

"That's because I don't *let* them!" Helen kicks a spray of water at the bank.

Moll doesn't respond but slowly dries her arms with her skirt.

Helen is embarrassed by her outburst. Anger makes her no better than Moses. She is proud of her orderly heart, for it has come from years of training. Moll will learn, just as she has learned. She settles herself and looks at her friend again with a smooth brow. "When you become plantation manager, Moll, you can do as you like."

"Till then, breed me out."

"It's what we all do. You're being spoiled."

Moll waits to see if Helen will catch the absurdity, will take it back. She doesn't. "God will hate you for this," Moll says.

Helen drops a handful of skirt and slaps Moll's face, softly. She fights her way up the bank again and wrings out her wet dress. The two girls carry their shoes back to the big house, where they leave them by the back steps for Mrs. Randolph to clean.

Helen eats dinner in silence, alone. One hand ladles rabbit soup while the other pages through the latest receipts for flour, cotton, coffee. She must pay in advance for space on the ships that carry the kegs of turpentine to New England and the Caribbean for trade. After spending an hour with her needlework and another hour reading *The Progress of Sin* from the tract society, she undresses and crawls into bed by herself. Moll has begun to spend more nights away. Helen doesn't know where she goes, what friends or lovers she has, but she is angry at her absence. Angry because she herself is as fixed as a potted plant. Yet where would she go if she could wander? By tying Moll to marriage, she is keeping them both in the same soil, root-bound. She cannot decide if this is unkind.

Helen fixes on a line from her reading — *A good tree cannot bring forth evil fruit* — and repeats the sentence until it becomes a puddle of the day's impressions. Moses and Moll and the spring minnows. Her father's letter, her mother's voice. Her own wedding day. The ringing bells.

84

In the morning, Helen visits the acres, where the spring sap is running. Two men peel the bark away from the pine trunks, leaving them pale and nude, and a third comes behind them to carve angled grooves in the raw flesh. Her father calls them catface trees. The sap oozes from these cuts in a slow bleed. A wooden trough catches the resin, which the distillery will turn to turpentine. The forest rises naked from the ground for four feet, four feet of white skin, before the trunks sheathe themselves in bark again. Helen knows better than to run her fingers down those glittering cuts.

Are any of these men a man that Moll would marry? She watches them drive their blades into the bark, their backs wet in the sun. She allows herself to think for a few moments of hands around her own waist, and then asks the foreman if Moses is working on the acres today. He shakes his head without looking at her. Men of any color are beasts.

Her hem already muddied, she crosses the trickling creek that divides Long Ridge from Cogdell's land. The cabin, her church, is empty. A dead bough from Christmas lies in the corner. She crushes the pine needles between her fingers and smells them. She probably has not saved a single soul. The men and women who sit on these hard benches are merely seeking shelter. She had a child's arrogance in starting this congregation, but no mission. Their bodies have been a grace to her. Who is a grace to them? They cannot keep a fire in this room, and still they come, even in winter. Rest, release. They come to her to be alone, sitting with their thoughts, while she seeks them out for the reflection of companionship. God is merely the lack of a whip.

She throws the dead branch outside and walks home.

The marriage takes place in the summer, among the heaved-up roots of the live oak, the lone tree that curves over the front lawn, bent and contorted to the shapes the easterly wind made. Moll fidgets in a yellow linen dress with two petticoats and holds a spray of goldenrod that she pulled from the back garden; no one else had thought to. One of the vestrymen from St. Paul's, whose roof is losing its shingles, shifts from one foot to another before the two negroes and mumbles out the service. Helen thanks him afterward with a piece of the groom's cake, and he bows and heads straight back to town with the crumbling slice in his hand. Asa is absent, accompanying a load of lumber to a new-built fort on Cape Lookout, eleven miles south. He told Helen to do as she liked, so she strung white muslin banners among the outbuildings behind the house, and here a little band sits and tunes, and a few of her pupils from the negro church gather silently. She demands merriment, and the newlyweds comply with a country dance. One old woman begins to clap her hands while two men slip away, back to their Sunday rest.

Helen cuts Mrs. Randolph's cakes and serves the slaves on china plates. Several guests sit on the ground to rest their saucers safely. A few speak a low-pitched language that is not English. Helen engages Miss

Kingston, who has brought her beau; the three of them will dine together after the festivities. The young man is from Wilmington and refuses his piece of cake, assuming it is a negro dish. When he is seeking out the housekeeper for a cloth to clean his boots, Helen asks Miss Kingston if she'd wish for a marriage herself.

"With Frederick?" She delicately sucks the icing off her fork tines. "My dear."

The women lean against the back staircase, and the white wood warms them through their dresses with residual sun. Helen has mostly stopped attending the schoolhouse now that she's busy with more important things; as the manager of the town's largest turpentine plantation, she deserves some acknowledgment, certain confidences.

"Are these a happy couple?" The older woman gestures toward Moll and Moses, who are sitting on a bench a few feet away, silent.

"Happy in God's eyes, certainly," Helen says. "Duty done."

"Mr. Foushee has fine prospects," Miss Kingston says. Despite being almost thirty, she has a habit of flaunting her position.

"You're fortunate he's not fighting."

Miss Kingston doesn't respond, and Helen realizes her error. There is unspoken shame here that the women maneuver around. These days, a man without a gun is hardly a man.

Helen takes Miss Kingston's arm and strolls her to a little gazebo that her mother had envisioned and her father had built after her death. They sit on the warping white boards and smooth their skirts, adjust the braids in their hair. Miss Kingston's little lace cap has migrated to the side of her head, and Helen straightens it. "I played here as a girl," she says, feeling sleepy and dull. It was hard to arrange for the wedding by herself, and she'll get no thanks from Moll.

"When were you a girl?" Miss Kingston asks. "You've been the boss of us all since you began coming to the schoolhouse."

She smiles, taking a compliment where it may not have been intended. "I suppose one takes the place that requires filling."

"I've always mourned for you, Helen, not having a mother, though I can't find any fault in you that would betray the lack. If I wished one thing for you, it would have been a little imagination." Through the screen of rambling clematis, the women can see the lap of ocean against the shore, the sea's slow breaths coming to them as a soft rustle. "Some of the negroes can read now. Perhaps you should leave them to teach the others. And now that Moll's got a partner, you can find your own path as a lady and a Christian. They'll need to learn to fear you."

Standing up impatiently, Helen catches the back of her skirt in a cluster of wooden splinters and tugs at the fabric. "I am more than grateful for your guidance and instruction, and I wish you and Mr. Foushee all happiness, but I already have a path for myself. It has been marked by necessity and the grace of God. Though I end my life a spinster, this plantation will be richer for it, and heaven will have its due."

Miss Kingston removes herself from the gazebo and deploys her parasol. "A spinster? Then your little farm will be sold at auction, parceled out to yeomen."

The shade of the heavy vines gives Helen a chill.

Frederick has reemerged from the house, boots shining, and is tapping his cane to the fiddler's rhythm, pretending not to search for his companion. Miss Kingston finds him, puts a hand on his arm, and gives him a look of gratitude.

Helen's shoes are loud in the slave cabin, which is nothing but a box made of boards. The cradle she has brought makes the room look smaller. An empty cradle in an empty home.

"At least take a rug from our house."

Moll is bent over, pulling at a loose plank in the floor. "I can make what I need," she says. Moses is absent for the housewarming.

Helen waits for Moll's fury. She will ask why Helen did nothing to stop this marriage and is leaving her alone in a house with a stranger. Helen would be terrified to be so abandoned, but what can she say? The lives around her are mapped by a higher hand, and she has learned to trust this. If she began now to doubt, if she studied unhappiness rather than duty, she might find her own life vulnerable. It hurts to see the people she loves in pain; she has no guarantee, after all, of God's promises. But she tells Moll to hold on because Helen is holding on too. They are all waiting for whatever will redeem them. And isn't the world, on the whole, a beautifully drawn thing? Can't she count back generations, through people that lived and begat life, to arrive at Adam himself? If this marriage is an evil, she hopes it's a small one.

Helen walks out to the porch, where breathing is easier. An old woman is returning from the fields, an empty pitcher in her hand. She doesn't look at Helen but keeps her head back, scanning the sky as if for Gabriel.

Helen has borne her share of small evils. She grew up motherless after all. Would she change this if she could? She sits on the edge of the porch, her feet brushing the tall grass. Would she ask God to provide a mother? Her hand combing through the girl's hair, catching out the knots. Her counsel at all the hard turns of Helen's life. Asa has not given her enough pieces to hold on to, so what she imagines is fiction. The only object she has is her mother's Bible; as a child learning to read, she translated God's word into her mother's voice. Faith was bequeathed to her. When she envisions the woman who bore her, she sees Mary and Martha and Ruth and Esther.

She feels a hand on her head.

Moll gives her two soft pats, and Helen doesn't know if this is scolding or reassurance. "Give me one of your nice brooms," she says.

"Is that all you want?"

"I wouldn't mind if I had some say in who I laid down with."

Helen nods. She puts her chin in her hands, nodding. People want what isn't given to them. And this is not sin, but hope.

What if God didn't put us here to accept, but to struggle? Isn't love itself built of that precise impossible hope?

When Moll sits down, Helen reaches out and holds her. Moll does not respond to the embrace but waits. Helen digs her fingers into Moll's back.

The next Sunday, she stands before three rows of black faces and tells them the shepherd's story. She reminds them that God loves each soul in his flock, that though a woman may find herself bound to heavy weights, God has not abandoned her, but will seek her and will find her. Helen asks Moll to read aloud.

Moll comes to the front of the room and opens her Bible. The other slaves who have learned to read follow along, trailing the words with their fingers.

"What man of you," she says, "having a hundred sheep, if he lose one of them, does not leave the ninety and nine in the wilderness, and go after that which is lost, until he find it?" She looks up and Helen nods. "And when he hath found it, he layeth it on his shoulders, rejoicing." Moll closes the book, puts it on the altar, and walks out of the makeshift church.

At eighteen, Helen has already rejected two suitors, one of whom was just home from war, legless. Asa introduced the men to her. They had each sat in the parlor, and Mrs. Randolph, whose children were beginning to be wed themselves, brought them a tray of sweets. From his desk across the hall, Asa could hear that Helen was polite and attentive. He saw her burn their letters in a bucket behind the house.

After Helen — who is perhaps more wealthy than beloved — dismisses the last visitor, she bids her father good night and slips down the back stairs, through the rangy garden, and across the creek. Asa watches from his window. Moll sleeps now in her husband's house on Cogdell's plantation, squeezed among the houses of other slaves. She has become less of a companion, more of a housemaid. He knows his daughter still seeks her out some nights for discussion. These are the times he considers moving his family to a proper town, one with more than a handful of oyster men and halfhearted farmers. But if ensuring his daughter's marriage requires abandoning his empire, then what good is empire? He is building something to last. The pine farms to the north are already sending their resin to his distillery.

A local regiment is returning to Beaufort for the summer to shore up the defenses along the sound. The fort to the south at Cape Lookout has been dismantled for lack of funds and ammunition, and the Continental Line is aware of the coast's vulnerabilities. With the additional men, Asa has more confidence about husband-catching. The fellow needn't be more than simply respectable. Helen already possesses the bounty.

Asa sets aside his accounts. Outside the window, the stars mimic his candle's flicker. He is older now than his father ever was.

A letter from his friend Colonel Ward of the Carteret County militia contains a few useful names, bachelors of good character, though men of their age were not meant to be matchmakers. Helen has grown headstrong in these years of his intermittent absence, and she may not suit an ordinary man. It's as well she's kept herself from novels.

In the morning, he'll call on William Dennis's mother, a widow who could not object to a visitor bearing a small bag of coffee and news from the Assembly. These soldiers all have sweethearts, of course, but Asa is objective enough to rate his daughter's beauty highly. He should really have a portrait done of her, to catch the brown curls and small, flowery mouth before she begins to fade. He and the widow will discuss weather and the war, and he will mention his daughter's pious ministrations and her health; Widow Dennis will remark to her battle-worn son on the benefit of an association. Seeds are easily planted — the reaping is the challenge.

Asa's mind rests on a plan like a man on a raft; it keeps him from the deeper waters. By the time he blows out his candle, the wax of which has pooled into a sort of continental map, he has forgotten about his daughter's night walk and anticipates his bed with pleasure.

In the summer of 1780, the ragged North Carolina regiments are tufts of themselves. The Beaufort soldiers are ashamed to be returning to their coastal home for this assignment, and relieved. Their brothers-in-arms have surrendered Charles Town to the British, and they have a sense that they are children in a man's game. Some board in the public house, others with kin. The embellished invitation to a gentlewoman's welcoming tea, while vaguely embarrassing, is a pleasure to receive.

Mrs. Easton, the colonel's mother, enlists the eligible young women of Beaufort to provide decorations for the event — a few doilies snatched from dowry chests and whatever flowers have survived the swamping heat of July. Helen brings rose mallow and yellow tickseed, feeling bridal. She is well aware of her father's gentle scheming but has no plans for conquest. Her passions are not yet directed toward love.

The soldiers arrive in a group and stand stiffly while Colonel John Easton kisses his mother. Bows are exchanged. Moll and another girl serve cakes and berries with averted eyes. Helen believes that her conversations with Moll are becoming less welcome, and when the slave passes her with a pitcher of lemonade, Helen pinches her on the leg. Moll slaps at her hand.

"Is it time for a song?" Mrs. Easton asks, spreading her hands out to suggest ease and plenty. She is small and topped with tight gray curls. "Eliza? Helen?"

Helen demurs, and so must listen to Eliza, a former schoolmate, bang out a hornpipe on the harpsichord while the soldiers practice their attentive looks. She is perched on a low chaise by the window and can angle her head toward the day outside while appearing contemplative. During the applause for Eliza, a young man standing behind Helen leans down and says, "Lovely." She nods without turning to look at him. The skin on the back of her legs goes cold.

94

As the entertainment progresses and the men begin to converse, Helen takes her turn and plays a slow piece by Scarlatti, inspecting the men in the corner behind the chaise. Young men look alike to her, and the artificiality of this gathering makes her wary. She has been conditioned to solitude. Even if she found a man to love — in the way that love is usually described — she doesn't know that she could enjoy it. Perhaps she wouldn't have understood this if she hadn't been placed on a harpsichord bench in a room full of lusting men and women, their hands twitching with the hope of the unexpected, but here she is, a girl who thinks in increasingly small orbits, thrust into a miniature of the world. She has no plans; she only knows that home, crop, and God are not plan enough.

In the late afternoon, when the tide is up and the town smells less like fish, Mrs. Easton herds the party onto the lawn. Some claim the scattered benches, others venture into the peach orchard, and a few young men stand by the front door, waiting for their colonel to claim them. Helen faces the sea, wondering if she'll be found again.

Mrs. Easton is at her side. "Darling, I want to present — here, step forward — William Dennis, the widow Dennis's son, though of course you may remember. Fighting for four years and a true patriot, with wounds to prove it. Your father — well, no need to be shy. I'll leave the pair of you, and very handsome-looking too." She unclasps her hand from the young man's arm and glances around for another opportunity to intervene.

"Welcome home," Helen says. The boy can't be more than nineteen, his face pimpled, his eyes permanently widened by war. "You sat in Miss Kingston's school for a short time, I believe."

"Yes, ma'am."

"Please. Helen."

"Your father's well?"

"Yes," she says. "And your mother?"

William clears his throat and joins his hands behind his back, as if it were a trick to appear older. "I'd be glad to call on you. During our stay." His eyes are too pale to be blue.

"How's the fighting been?"

"Oh!" He laughs, surprising himself. "Not for ladies' ears."

Helen turns back toward the sea. "I imagine one finds religion quickly on the battlefield."

"Not so much religion, ma'am, as faith in men."

"With a thousand aiming to kill you?"

"Well. There are those who'd pull you out of ditches, no fear for their own skin."

"Don't you think of death?"

He reaches for his chest to hold on to his musket strap, but of course he's left it at his mother's house. "It's present always, so we don't mind it. Just a little step between that path and ours."

"And you're not afraid of that little step?"

"We all take it, ma'am."

As dusk is covering the peach trees, the soldiers return their empty glasses and the women smooth their stomachers. In dim corners, parting words are exchanged. Helen has found her way back to the chaise in the parlor, which has yet to be lamp-lit. She is waiting to walk home with Moll and ask her what it's like to be married to a man such as Moses, what it's like to be married at all. What are the mysteries? Though of course there was no choice. Any fear that Helen has, Moll must have had too. If she were better at admitting fault, she would feel some guilt in this. What is a life without the ability to choose? This over that; him, or not him. Moll's life is not so distant from Moll's death.

A man sits down beside her. He looks like any other soldier. He speaks to her in a calm, low voice, like a man to a horse. "William Dennis says he's to be your husband."

"Not so at all," she says.

"The bride of Dennis," he says, "who launched a thousand ships."

"No, nor burned any topless towers." She stands. She wants to be indignant. "You're a bit fine-read for a soldier."

"Got my start on Goodrich's boat. A rather literary man."

"The pirate?" she asks. "And you dare stand among American men?"

He rises from the sofa and looks at her with his head to one side. Helen is caught between curiosity and shame. "I'll bring you to sail one day. Wherever you like."

She shakes her head. "I get seasick."

"Are you afraid?"

His eyes grow deeper the longer she looks at them. "I can't swim," she says.

"So say the faint of heart." He turns toward the door and gathers his cap from the hall stand. Helen follows him. Through the open door, they can hear Mrs. Easton's noisy farewells. Helen puts out her hand to stop him. It is almost night, and she can still see him perfectly. He waits, her hand almost on his arm.

CHAPTER
FOUR

She sits on the edge of the sofa so her feet can touch the ground. Her skirts, patterned in a red floral stripe, balloon over her knees and hang just above the satin points of her shoes. She has only recently become conscious of the female artifice. William Dennis perches on a chair across from her and fiddles so much with his cup that his saucer fills with tea. Though the windows are open and they can hear a breeze lifting the leaves outside, the room feels close.

"The regiment leaves next week," he says.

Helen's mind crawls in slow circuits. She drags her civility to the surface. "And will you miss Beaufort?" This is the wrong question.

"I will certainly miss its beauties," William says. He dips his head forward, signaling, but looks like a puppy searching for a teat.

"We are all proud to have you elsewhere, though. Your heroism is best practiced on a larger scale." She pauses to let him work out a reply. "I'm sure your mother will miss you."

"And you?" His cheeks are red in patches.

"I pray nightly for all our soldiers." She stands and tries to shake out her skirt, which catches in folds over the rough fabric of her petticoats. The costume of young women is altogether absurd. Yet even in this interview, Helen strives to appear beautiful. She is aware of the escaping curls that frame the base of her neck, and when she holds out her hand to mark the tea's conclusion, she looks forward to William's bewilderment when he presses her soft fingers.

"May I come again before I leave?" he asks, her hand still caught in his.

"We would never turn you away, Captain Dennis."

The graveyard by the church is hemmed by a low stone wall, and in the afternoon the sun comes through the oaks in slowly moving disks. A wind sends them brushing along the tops of headstones. The graves are arranged in scattered clusters around the cemetery, kin with kin. The mockingbirds hop through the canopy of hollies and cedars, but the ground is empty of bird life and cooler than any other shade.

"Do you think we're feeling ghosts?" John asks. He stands by a row of small markers, their size corresponding to the age of the dead.

Helen, several steps ahead, turns. "It's only cooler because of all the stone. I didn't take you for superstitious."

Their voices seem out of place here. He worries that they will never find the words for each other.

John had called on her father today, introduced himself briefly, and asked Helen for a walk. Both father and daughter looked skeptical. But she had come, and they had spoken little. He took her from Long Ridge down the oak-lined road to town, along Front Street where the voices of fishermen filled their own silence, and back in a loop down Ann Street. He would not have taken her through a cemetery if she had not asked.

If he tried to say what drew him to her, he would only find a handful of gestures. Her first refusal to perform on the harpsichord; her focus beyond the window in a room crowded with friends and strangers; her glances, which were as direct and unblinking as a hawk's. The feeling of her hand an inch from his arm. He does not consider himself a lonely man, and yet he needs something in her gaze. Honesty, perhaps, or conviction.

John came to Beaufort as an ex-pirate and a soldier, not a son, not a brother. His youth was spent inland — without the breath of the ocean — where his cousin's farm melted into the fields of other farmers. There was little worth owning. He had no mother or father to hold him and tell him he was precious; he had nothing to love in return. There had been idle friends, neighbor girls, the woman who cooked his meals, but never someone like this. Someone who belonged.

John waits as Helen examines a grave that looks like the others. A vaulted tomb, low, covered over in brick. Looking down a row of these half cylinders humping from the ground, he gets the impression of a sea serpent, or a row of waves.

"They look like cannon," she says, following his eyes.

He looks up. Of course they do.

"Have you any family here?" she asks.

A circle of sun is sliding across her face, brushing her shoulder. He is drawn to the softness within her practiced husk, the sadness that led her to her mother's grave; now he can read the name on the stone. He is drawn to the part of her that will never tell him this is her mother's grave. The fear inside her fearlessness.

He sits on one footstone and she sits on another and he gives her a sketch of his childhood, from his parents' death to the crowded mattress in his cousin's home. "I can't imagine visiting a place like this to look for family. I suppose I've been told that when they're gone, they're gone."

"It wouldn't be a comfort to find them again?"

"The past is not particularly interesting to me," he says. Life is what's ahead of him. These monuments around them don't call to mind the bodies beneath. They are merely stones over dirt, stools on which a person can sit. The lack of birds does not actually alarm him; his talk of ghosts had been a reach for the romantic in her. Perhaps her denial had a similar intent.

He looks over, imagining now this mutual impulse of theirs, and waits for her to turn to him with a response in her eyes.

Instead, she stands, brushes off her skirt, and holds out her hand for him to shake. "Thank you for the expedition," she says, and before he can respond, he is alone in the graveyard.

Two days later, he is at her door again. Helen refuses to walk with him. She cannot always say yes, and she is tired from lack of sleep. Sleep lost to thoughts of him.

She takes him across the lawn to the water's edge, where a yaupon holly hangs over a rowboat run aground. They climb in and sit on the thwarts, facing each other.

"Shall I row us?" he asks.

Helen cannot determine what about this person draws her. He is not plantation management, not father, not church. There is nothing familiar about him. At night, when she should be dreaming, she has worked him over like a puzzle. Maybe it is simply having something to think about. He could be the grit that she will worry until it becomes a pearl, beloved.

"Where would you like to go?"

"If this boat were in the water?" Helen's imagination is weak, only because she has never wanted something desperately.

"I'll take you to Barbados. You should've brought a hat to keep the sun off."

"What will you do when the war is over?"

He pulls in the dry oars. His face is open and clear, as though he has no attachments, and thus no guilt. This openness is hypnotic. She finds herself wanting to brush her fingers across his forehead.

"I'll find a job somewhere, or a bit of farm," he says.

"You could ferry young ladies from place to place."

He shakes his head. "Too dangerous. My heart is susceptible enough on dry land." He rolls up the sleeves of his shirt and leans forward, his elbows on his knees. "What about you? What will you do when you put down your gun?"

"I should like to see a little of the world. Do the things I have not yet done. And then I should like to be a vicar."

She has never had such pleasure from making a man laugh, and it is not a feeling of conquest, as she might have thought, but surrender. When he laughs, she wants to swim into him. She knows that his pleasure is not in her dream's absurdity, but in its aptness.

There are no bodies to haunt them in this boat beneath the holly. When John holds his hand out, he's surprised that she takes it. Her smile when they touch is unexpected.

The note Asa receives from Widow Dennis is not accusatory, only concerned. Her boy shows signs of melancholy. She told William how women lead men with a string through the forests of love, but her son cannot read any hope in Helen's flirtations. Asa folds the letter into squares. So perhaps the boy isn't in love after all. He tosses the little packet on his desk, where it splays open again. Love breeds delusion.

Asa knows his daughter has begun to keep her heart a secret. He has bribed Moll for hints, but there are things a father will never know. Was his own wife's father cut off like this? He could confront her, take away her inheritance for any whispers of an unsuitable match, but that would be doing himself no favors. There are no other heirs, only distant cousins who wouldn't move to a shrinking town on the nubbin of North Carolina. Years of war, of ship-building and ship-sinking, have turned his farm into a business; he

104

could sell it all if he were offered some governmental post, give Helen the money, abandon his trees for the oversight of citizens. But then why has he had a family? What will remain of him on this earth when his flesh molders? If there is a heaven, what will he look down to see?

If there is a heaven, he has made no provisions for it.

Whether it's fortune or a governorship for Asa, his daughter won't marry a parentless privateer. He has created dignity out of thin air, his own grandparents being no more than laborers, immigrants to an open land. He has claimed a stake now and will not regress. William Dennis's kin brought Africans to this coast and turned plots of cabbage into acres of rice. William Dennis's kin have left a visible streak through the darkness of the past.

He pushes the folded note aside and retrieves a fresh sheet of paper from his desk. With an unsteady quill, he begins, "Most excellent lady."

In the last of the day's light she slips down to the marsh's edge, frightening off a cloud of plovers. John is waiting, silhouetted against pale violet, jabbing a stick into the mud. She stops before the ground grows moist and waits for him to turn. They play the game in which he inches toward her, swallowing the space between them, measuring her stillness, until she laughs and spins away, reclaiming distance. He has come within a foot of her.

"I'll tell you more of my pirating days, and then you won't miss me."

"Don't," Helen says. "I'll turn you in."

"We'd kidnap captains' wives and use their finery as fish bait. Many a time I cut my finger setting ribbon and lace on hooks."

She holds up her hand, and he raises his so they can feel the warmth between them. "Your stories are all the more wicked for being false," she says.

He throws his stick into the sound, where it floats. "Do you mean to encourage William Dennis?"

"He's a friend of my father's."

"He knows I see you sometimes."

"You mention it, do you?" She wishes she had brought the little folding chair. Her body is tired. She begins to walk back toward the house.

"He asked me to speak well of him. To mention his merits to you."

"Proceed," she calls back.

"I will not court you for my brother."

Helen stops. In the distance, she can make out the opening faces of the moonflower she planted to creep up the front steps of Long Ridge. She turns around, and John has not moved. For two weeks, they have traded stories of sea and land but have built no castles. There have been no promises. If asked what she wants, perhaps Helen could not answer coherently. She wants to do right, above all, and the man in his summer uniform, heat radiating from his fingertips, does not fit with what she has been told is the purity of love.

And yet they are undoubtedly courting, even in the absence of words. Whether she is hungry for him because he is a man and she is lonely, or whether she is hungry for *him*, she is bound now. He approached her as a friend, reminding her how few of these she has. She has begun to understand that her life is small, and she cannot accept smallness.

She continues on to the house, not responding.

Helen wakes with the feeling of a deep concavity in her abdomen: giddiness. The soldiers are mustering today in the field north of town, but there is no everyday course that will take her walking past them. She gathers her needlework in a bag instead, and visits the store that stands two blocks from the church. She leans against the wooden counter as the boy in the apron tries to match her thread. He holds up a yellow that looks like summer weeds, and she says, "Paler."

When Moll comes in, head down, Helen turns to look away. There is hardly any need for awkwardness; the women have not seen each other since Mrs. Easton's tea, but there has been no argument, only the growing up that happens so much faster at this age than at any other. Helen in the third week of July is a stranger to Helen in June. Moll stabs her with a finger as she passes, and Helen gives a little leap of surprise.

The boy has wrapped her thread in paper and has tried to sell her a broom, and now Helen lingers outside with her parcel, waiting for Moll.

"You haven't any money to buy things," she says when Moll comes out empty-handed.

"Will soon. I asked him if he'd take eggs to sell and he didn't see why not."

"Where'd you get chickens from?"

Moll takes the thread from her hand and peels back the paper to see what color she chose. "Moses is what we call a finder." Helen begins to walk home, and Moll takes a half skip to catch up to Helen's pace, thrusting the thread back at her. "Mending?"

"A fire screen, I expect," Helen says. She concentrates on her steps, directing the fall of her feet, heel and ball, careful to avoid kicking dust on her dress. "I can't imagine you'll get more than a few shillings for your eggs. You'll be wanting to buy your freedom soon." It is hot, and she'd rather be thinking of other things.

"You have a way of laughing at me." Moll stops in front of the church and Helen turns around, impatient. "But you're the one hasn't done anything at all."

Helen opens her mouth to say the dozen things she has accomplished that day alone, not the least of which is finding the yellow thread to suit the warblers in her pasture scene, but Moll has a hand around her arm now.

"You've just been playing at hearts." She gives another tickle under Helen's arm, and Helen pushes her away.

"When I wish to discuss love with you, Moll, I will certainly inform you, but I have no inclination for it when you act like a child." She turns for home again. The paper around the thread, clenched in her fist, is damp now, and she ignores her steps long enough to turn her hem red with dust. She hears Moll behind her, and she is sorry for her anger. Tomorrow she will have to sit in that church and listen to a layman describe God's mercy, or his wrath, and it will take all her strength to recall the fervor she had for Jesus. She is worried enough about her heart without Moll examining it.

Two men pass on the other side of the road; they look at her and nod. She sees what they see: a white woman running away from a slave. One spending money for woven silk, the other pocketing pence for eggs. She slows to signal to Moll her forgiveness. The other woman slows too, maintaining the distance. When they have reached the green alley leading to Long Ridge, out of any man's earshot, Helen stops. She does not face Moll but knows she is listening, the shadow behind her.

"I don't want to marry."

"Neither did I."

"That's entirely different."

Moll laughs. "It sure turned out to be."

When Helen looks at her, the sun is cutting across her face through the oaks, turning triangles of her dark skin golden. "Do you want me to apologize?"

"Sometimes I wish you would talk to me," Moll says. "And sometimes I wish you would leave me alone. Doesn't matter much what I'd rather."

"You didn't say a word to me at the soldiers' tea."

"I took your glass from you when you were done." Moll swats at a horsefly that has begun to circle her head.

"Will you come inside? Mrs. Randolph is squeezing lemons."

"Yes, I will gladly be served by a white woman." Moll tries to smile. "You want me to carry your thread? Lift your dress up from the road so it doesn't get dirty?"

"Don't be rude. I miss you, and I'm too tired to play cat and mouse. Come tell me whether this color will do." The two women walk side by side toward the white house at the end of the alley. "I've done the meadow with the rabbits, but I can't get the sky right. I thought it looked too empty, and now I fear it will be overrun with birds."

His parents having died when he was young, and himself having been raised by impoverished cousins in a village outside of Beaufort's orbit, John sees love, or rather desire, as a gift the world offers, to be claimed like any other. His nights, at first, are not sleepless. His breath is not disturbed. He remembers Helen's face clearly, even the tapering corners of her eyes, and does not spend his hours between musters trying to recapture her features. While William Dennis still languishes, John must be silent, and the lack of a confidant does not trouble him. He is a man who takes things as they are given to him.

He only feels discomfort when William Dennis sits beside him on his cot in Widow Dennis's house, for they are sharing William's old bedroom, and asks him how to win a woman's love. John has had few opportunities in his life for deceit. He speaks to him of courage and patience and avoids the subject of resignation, which is at every road's end, without which the world would have long since died of grief.

"Haven't you any sweetheart?" William asks.

"There was a girl before I enlisted."

"She let you kiss her?"

Had John wanted to kiss her? When he thinks of her face, he sees Helen's. "She brought scones to my cousin's house, each with a *J* written in currants."

"She would have been sorry to see you go. She's the type who'd send you letters."

There are no letters. Thinking on it, he had never given her encouragement, though he would have kissed her. He hadn't given her anything in return, and for the first time, he imagines the girl at home, brokenhearted. She is not sending letters because she wants him to feel her lack, to punish. And he has not felt anything at all, has not noticed until William Dennis, with his lion's heart, has come to her defense. Could anyone leave Helen so abandoned? "I don't know what women would do without their letters," John says.

Neither is an unhandsome man. William is thinner, his eyes lighter and more vulnerable. "I believe her father supports my cause," he says.

"Any parent would."

"Then you think I should ask."

The sun through the south window falls upon the back of John's neck. He had wanted to sleep this afternoon. His nights have become Helen's. William would have made her a moon goddess by now, would have translated her paleness into an angelic affinity. John has never regretted his lack of sentimentality, but perhaps women wish for some servitude. He has doubts where he had none. "What does her face look like when you speak to her?"

"She is all kindness," William says.

"Melting eyes?"

"I think she is too much a lady to betray herself."

Helen's arms last night. John does not want to think of her; he wants to sleep. He lies back on the cot, folding his legs behind William, who still looks into his open hands. "Could you live without her?" John asks, eyes closed.

"Could anyone?"

He is still sane enough not to dream of her, or not to remember his dreams. When he wakes, William is gone. One of his legs has gone numb. Soldiers are useless in Beaufort. Where will he go when the war is done? Take his commission, buy a farm, learn to farm. He cannot return to sea with a wife. Her arms are like the sea. He rubs the sleep out of his eyes. There is no way in which her arms are like the sea.

"You never act like yourself anymore," Helen says. They sit in the parlor, surrounded by low cushioned chairs and the painted ladies on the wallpaper that beckon to the painted men. Helen has hung a crucifix on the wall above one of Asa's desks as a rebuke. The figure's doleful eyes observe her struggles; his wounds remind her that he is an ally. She is glad Moll followed her home from the store because now they can forgive each other.

Moll rests her lemonade on her knee, rubbing the imprinted glass with one finger. The bottom of the glass is wet from washing, and it leaves a dark ring on her skirt. "I suppose you know me better than anyone, is that it? You who wouldn't care if I was married to a monster or sold to Georgia."

112

"Is it this house? You're not comfortable here."

"Oh, too grand for the likes of me?"

"Very well," Helen says, standing up. "I see we won't make any progress." She reaches for Moll's glass. "Give it here."

"I'm not done."

"You're too busy mocking me." She grabs the glass from Moll's hand. "I'll tell Mrs. Randolph you found it too sweet. Up, up. We're going outside." Helen clears the room of dishes. She is tired of having her intentions judged and misjudged.

By the shore the grass is dry. They have not had an afternoon thunderstorm in days, and some of the weeds are singed from the heat. Helen lies down on her back and digs her fingers into the dry dirt. Moll stands beside her, scuffing the toe of her slipper along the ground. Her hands rest on her waist, and she squints to filter this scene: the sun mirroring off the water, the white woman in her white dress ablaze on the ground, a lizard shimmying down the marsh reeds, stopping to puff out its red neck. There are no clouds for cover. A schooner is slack-sailed beyond the opening to the sound. Windless, the land buzzes and waits.

Moll sits beside Helen, taking a handful of the other woman's dress and smoothing its folds between her fingers, admiring the linen. Helen's eyes are closed, and she smiles at this touch.

"Why must you hold everything against me?" she says.

Moll lets the fabric drop and lies back on the grass next to her. "You think you're in love?"

113

Helen rises up on her elbows. A dragonfly is wavering over Moll's shoulder, dipping as if to drink. "It seems a luxury, don't you think?"

"I wouldn't have thought anything was a luxury to you. You snap a gold spoon and your daddy hands you another."

"Gold spoons." Helen laughs and falls back again. She had never minded the North Carolina heat, for it was always tinged with this spark of salt. Opening her mouth, she can taste the weather. If called upon to travel, by a husband perhaps, Helen would embark willingly. She is young enough to adore her home and to leap at whatever is not her home. But in her years of girlhood, she has defined her duty narrowly: she owes her service to her father and her slaves, to the turpentine business and to the catface trees behind Long Ridge. She is a servant of God, whose scope is small.

"Which soldier is it?" Moll says.

"Would you say you love Moses?"

"Now you believe marriage is about love?"

"Father made that match. I had nothing to do with it."

"You sure saw it through."

A feather, some tuft of egret down, tumbles up the bank and settles against Helen's hand, making her start. Her chest grows warm with unhappiness.

"There were no women out on your ships, I suppose," William says, gnawing the meat off the bone of chicken.

Widow Dennis brings in a platter of rice and onions. "Yes, tell us stories of pirates, John. Give them a better name."

"I was hardly pirating," John says. Two other men from the regiment have joined Widow Dennis's table to avoid the army's cauldrons of rabbit stew. They repay the widow's generosity by eating in silence. John spoons some rice onto his plate. "I manned sails, coiled rope, scrubbed boards. Took a turn as cook."

"Never killed a man?" William asks.

"Can't say." John smiles. "Through the smoke, I never saw the cannonballs land."

"Did you travel far, John?" The widow has eaten nothing. After the men leave for the evening march, she will collect their scraps and make a plate for herself. She has not gotten rich by wasting food.

"To any island you can imagine. I've seen more monsters than women."

"You would've wooed them all," she says. She looks around at the men at her table. "Be careful of your handsome faces, my boys. Don't let the British near them. We'll have little else after this fight." Widow Dennis has already buried her plated silver under the holly tree. She winks at her son.

John does not touch her. At most, they stand side by side and look out together, assessing the ocean. They find points on the horizon and imagine traveling there: the West Indies, Charles Town, the sandy shoals that stand between Beaufort and the Atlantic. John tells her there was once a fort on Bogue Island, to the west of the inlet where ships come through, built to protect the town from Indians and anyone else with a cause, but the army never finished the southern wall. The fort was made of bundles of sticks tied and stacked like firewood, and it is true that this might stop a musket ball, but cannon would have scattered the battery as easily as kindling. She says, You think of the world in terms of what it will withstand; he does not yet know how she thinks of the world. They imagine building a home in the wreckage of the fort.

They have sat next to each other, and the edge of her skirt has fallen on his crossed knee. He remembers these moments but does not dwell. He has no need to think of them often. But he has not thought of marrying her either; he has assumed they will always meet at night in unplanned places and share some silence. Family life is not something he's been fitted for. And if William Dennis asks her? She'll say yes; that's what women are accustomed to do. And then, when he is ready and less awed, he won't be able to reach out for her arm. She'll be married and using that arm to hold her children.

At the end of the summer, the regiment folds its uniforms and fills its sacks with meal for the road. William Dennis has bent his head in the garden of Long Ridge and asked for Helen's whole heart. He has found solace in his mother, who made him a pudding with the last of her sugar. He shared the treat with John and the two other men, and they cursed women together and let the night slide away in drink when the pudding was gone. In the morning, William had finished combing his hair before he remembered. He then lay down, brokenhearted, until dinner.

On their last day in Beaufort, the soldiers say their parting words. Mrs. Easton's home is busy with grateful men, and a few young ladies host those men who have declared themselves stricken with love. They place ladyfingers on small china plates and wait for their mothers to leave them for a final kiss with their beau and a promise of letters. In the evening, John visits Helen.

"I don't expect you to write me," she says. They stand in the hall by the door. Since she first reached for his arm in Mrs. Easton's house, passageways have seemed romantic places. She does not let him into the parlor or offer him any sustenance. Their bodies fit shyly into a corner of the hall, just beyond the window's slant of moonlight. He takes two of her fingers in his hand, then three. She fidgets, listening for Asa's step on the stairs.

"I don't want you to wait," he says.

She pulls her hand back. It is hard to speak of feeling to a man who will soon be the target of British muskets. But she is young still, and danger, like all things, is transitory. She speaks with her head down.

"I want you to wait," she says. John doesn't reply, so she lifts her head and repeats herself. "Don't find anyone else."

He reaches for her waist and she pulls away.

"I don't know that I'll ever see you again," she says, "and I don't want any memory to linger over. I don't want to be kept up nights thinking of a kiss."

"It's like loving a ghost." He gently kicks her shoe with his.

It's the first time he has mentioned love, and she regrets it. She has always buffered her life against pain, and this is a new worm in the heart. "Don't promise that you'll come back."

"I'll come back," he says.

The darkness folds over him. All she can see, standing at the open door, is the glint of the moon on the moving sea.

Two days outside of Beaufort, the men pause in a meadow for their dinner. It is the middle of August, and they huddle around the trunks of pecan trees like cows. The commissary hands out salted fish and apples requisitioned from a farm. William Dennis's canteen is empty; he asks John for a sip from his.

"Your mother will be glad to see you settle in Beaufort again," John says. "After this is done. Save you from the shad." He eats his ration with his hands, for there is no juice left in the fish to be neat about.

"You think we'll make it home again?"

John stops eating. William is sitting with his knees pulled up, his back against the tree. He twists one foot slowly back and forth, scraping a fan in the dry dirt, and doesn't look at John. The men's coats are beside them, dust-colored from the summer. A bluebird shuffles among the branches above them, darting out for an insect in the open air and falling back into the pecan again.

"Did you speak to her before you left?" William asks.

"I did."

"Is it you she wants?"

John swallows the last bite of his fish. "It isn't our will that brings us to the battlefield and leaves us there or leads us away." John stands up and wipes his hands on his pants. "That's what's been told us. That's why we don't all hide under our beds. If there were no God, would you have left your mother's house?"

"If there were no God, I wouldn't have a mother at all."

The men begin to sort themselves for the afternoon's travels. From the other side of the tree, John can hear the smooth metal sounds of a man cleaning his gun.

Her shoes sit on the porch by the front door, their heels in clods of mud. Asa sits next to them in a straight-backed chair, turning from the view of his lawn to the empty shoes and back to the lawn. Colonel Easton once questioned its expanse, its British emptiness. "Grass is no crop I know of," he said, and Asa said, "But it looks well." It suggests leisure.

The shoes have been empty all afternoon. His daughter is closed in the parlor with a gentleman whom Asa believes is some sort of itinerant, but Helen has made him promise not to ask. "A merchant here on business," she said. This is his second day in the house, so what else could he be but a painter? There are ladies in New Bern having their miniatures done, and it was only a matter of time before the art arrived in Beaufort. Asa imagines his daughter's pose.

119

He digs at the ankles of his own shoes until they slide off, one landing on the buckle. The small clink sends a hawk bolting from the oak; it cuts across the breeze and then drifts back, watching the earth for movement. Asa stretches his socked feet, flexing his toes. A laugh spills out of a window. If she were being painted, shouldn't she be still? He'll put it on his desk, propped up behind his ledgers. When she gives him the little painting, he'll say, "But when did you have this done? What a secret-keeper!" He closes his eyes to better set the scene. He is ready to let her carry the weight of his endeavors, though it would calm him to have a grandson before settling his accounts. He doesn't know what happened with Widow Dennis's son. Young ladies these days are expected to find a little love in the match; no harm in that, if the lady is not unreasonable. Asa loved his wife. That is, he wished mostly to be near her; he looked on her with pleasure; and when she died, he felt the lack of her — felt it as an emptiness in his leg bones that made his walking hard.

Her parents had introduced them, just as he had pushed William Dennis Helen's way. They had sat politely in someone's drawing room and there had been a fascination on his part with the half-open window, through which he could observe freedom. His mother asked the girl questions, and she spoke so quietly that sometimes his mother said, "Pardon?" He would glance back into the room, and she would turn her eyes at him like a rabbit in the woods, and he would cough until his eyes watered. That was courtship.

He had no image of her, no ivory painting the size of a thumbnail or sketch drawn hastily on a summer's picnic. But there was an impression that lasted longer than ink. He did not have to see God's face to believe in him. There is a searing in the body's innards that never leaves; it's the thumbprint of the beloved, and its formlessness does not diminish its endurance. Like his wife, God has left him empty-handed, forsaken.

It is January, and the farm has quieted to a hum. Asa has hired his slaves out to the men clearing fields for rice. The pines are rebuilding their sap for the spring's cutting. Some mornings are warm, but on this one, Helen wakes to a web of frost on her window, through which the sea appears hazy and jagged. Downstairs, she helps Mrs. Randolph roll out flour for biscuits; they knead without speaking, their hands dusted white. A hired man walks across the back fields, and the sound of his feet on the hard grass reaches the women with their dough.

It is already 1782, a year and a half since Helen last saw John, and she has had only one letter, brief, with the smell of fighting on it.

I am in a tent with three other men, somewhere inland. We had meat on Sunday. Col. Ward has joined us and seems a just man. Daniel Foot is here, you'll remember his Beaufort cousins. He writes a sweetheart but won't tell who she is. Perhaps it's you. I haven't killed a man yet, I hope you're pleased to know.

She had taken pains only to read the letter twice before she folded it away, but it was not hard to remember. Her parsing of it revealed little. He may feel jealousy, he may desire her good opinion. Nothing more could be proven. She imagines slipping out of the house one morning and walking to wherever he is, across the miles of unknown. His face when he first spots her through the trees. Her hands pressing his neck, finding his ears. This is her beginning to imagine. But at twenty years old, she is still digging the heels of her palms into biscuit dough, the bread to be eaten only by her father.

Mrs. Randolph begins to whistle. Helen brushes away a strand of hair, wiping a streak of flour across her forehead, and leans against the wooden table.

"You needn't do more, miss."

"We're almost through. Hand me the jar." Helen presses circles in the dough. "Do you miss your husband, Mrs. Randolph?" He had died looking for free land on the frontier, shot through with a Cherokee arrow. His partner had buried him in the west and sent Mrs. Randolph his musket and his spectacles. The gun she keeps hung behind her cabin door, where all the little Randolphs know to find it.

"I mostly miss the money he brought in, to speak frankly. He was a good father to the little ones and did well by us, but there's something rather nice about one's own life. Making decisions without someone to tell you no, best not do that. He never thought I could do much for myself."

"We're lucky to have you," Helen says.

"There's no telling what all I can do without him, miss." She arranges the biscuits on a sheet and hangs them over the fire, where they already look golden in the light.

Helen carries a basket of the fresh-baked bread to the cabin where she leads prayer. Two elderly women sit on the front bench, and Moll sits behind them. Only when Helen sets the basket down on the altar and opens her mother's gilt-edged Bible does she see her father sitting in the back corner in a rush-bottomed chair, separate from the pews of the faithful. His arms are crossed.

She leads the slaves in the Lord's Prayer before asking them their catechism.

"What is your name?"

They each call out their name. Asa is silent.

"What is your duty toward God?"

They speak in a jumble. "To believe in him, to fear him, and to love him with all my heart, with all my mind, with all my soul, and with all my strength."

After the service, Helen walks with Moll back toward Long Ridge. She looks along the path for Asa, but he left when she was speaking to Aunt Caty about her grandson. Moll pauses when they reach the dividing creek, and there is a moment in which Helen feels like she is being asked to cross Styx alone, that every friend she's made in life will desert her before the final passage. She does not yet have Mrs. Randolph's resignation. Helen reaches for Moll's hand. "Come home," she says. "For a little while." She pulls her across the creek, and the grass in the late morning is once again soft under their feet. Helen's fingers tighten in Moll's.

When they come into the parlor, a sprig of holly in Helen's hair, Moll carrying her muddy shoes in one hand, Asa is sitting in a chair by the window. His coat is draped over his lap, and his hands are buried in its folds for warmth.

"Has no one put a fire in the room this morning?" Helen releases Moll and goes to call Mrs. Randolph.

Asa turns away from the window and looks at Moll. "Did you enjoy church this morning?"

"Your daughter is a fine speaker, sir."

"And do you believe in the answers you gave to the catechism?"

Moll looks at the sofa, and Asa nods his head. She sits. "The Lord does his best by us, sir."

"Even by you?" The older Asa gets, the more often he wishes he were asleep. Even now, he envies Moll the sofa, the possibility it provides of horizontal rest. The conversations he starts, he could slip away from unfinished, without any feeling of loss.

Helen returns to find them silent. She brushes at the dust on the mantel above the cold fireplace. In a moment, Mrs. Randolph arrives with wood under her arm and kneels on the stone flagging.

"Have you always been faithful to God?" Asa asks Helen.

She glances at Moll, who is tucking her bare toes under the Turkey rug.

"I mean since you were a child. I only wonder if you always had this faith."

124

"It was something my mother left me," Helen says.

"I should be getting home," Moll says, but does not stand.

Asa shakes his head. "What my father told me was that our lives are our own and only when we die do we hand them over to God and heaven."

"You don't think he has any say in our fortunes on earth?" Helen asks.

"I can't see how she would have left you with anything like faith, you not even knowing her."

"We choose what to take," Helen says.

"From people and God too," Moll says. Her feet are entirely under the rug, and she won't look at Asa.

"What do you take, Moll? I can't see you've been treated very well."

The fire has swallowed the cut wood now and Mrs. Randolph leaves the room with her head down, hoping not to be questioned on her faith.

"Helen says the Bible teaches us to be dutiful. I can see that's well enough for keeping people quiet and getting in the crops on time. And the reward lasts forever. I suppose I'm of your mind, sir, that God only comes in at the end."

"Why go to church?"

"We must know how to recognize him when he comes for us."

"If you lead a proper Christian life," Helen says, her fingers drumming on the mantel, "he's with you always. There's no end of one thing and beginning of another."

"Then what's heaven?" Moll asks.

125

Helen comes to sit next to her on the sofa. "It's just a greater closeness with God. Which is a reward, as you say."

"Do you believe you'll see your mother there?" Asa asks.

"It doesn't so much matter," she says. "It's not a place with real people."

"I thought you said it's whatever we can imagine," Moll says.

"Then you are not afraid of death," Asa says.

Helen looks from Moll to Asa. "I'm afraid of you dying. I'm afraid of being left alone. But I think after we die there's only goodness."

"I don't see why there can't be goodness before we die," Moll says.

"You think I should begin to pray?" Asa fiddles with a candlestick on the table by the window, picking at the dried wax on the silver.

Helen laughs. "What, you think I'd recommend against it?" She doesn't find any smile in his features. "I think God likes to hear his name being praised. He's a father, isn't he? And he always listens."

"Especially to white folks," Moll says. She removes her feet from the warmth of the rug and, after a short curtsy to Asa, grabs her shoes by the door and leaves the room.

Helen finds her struggling with her heavy gray coat on the back steps. Moths have eaten through the shoulders and the breast pocket. "I wanted to have a nice talk with you," Helen says. "I don't know what's

126

wrong with him. Perhaps in winter everyone thinks of the things they've lost."

Moll waits for a moment to see if Helen will continue, and then speaks into the silence. "I'm going to have a baby."

Helen grabs her wrist. "Moses's?"

"It'll join the rest of his little bastards."

"Moll, I'm so happy for you. Is it a good thing? I always find myself envious of you."

Moll buttons her coat, or those buttons that are left. She reaches up and strokes Helen's hair, which is coming loose from its pins on one side and which catches what little light sieves through the clouds. "Somehow I don't think your heaven will look anything like my life." She yanks the end of Helen's curls, then heads back toward home.

"Let me be its godmother," Helen calls after her.

"You can't even get your own daddy to pray!"

Moll looks like a heron crossing the fields with her skirts pulled up in a bunch around her shins, the tails of her coat flapping behind her. Helen cannot imagine such a thin bird becoming a mother.

That spring there is a sense that the Americans are winning. Since 1775, Asa has no longer sold his turpentine to the British, and now his gamble is paying off. War is good for his business, so he has been content to wait. In March, he receives a letter from the North Carolina General Assembly. They praise his industry, they flatter his loyalty, and they ask him to serve as the representative from Carteret County in the summer deliberations. He is ready for a larger role in the trajectory of his state, and Helen has proven herself more than capable of handling the daily operations in his absence.

When he tells her of his decision at supper that night, she congratulates him.

"They meet in Hillsborough now, so I'll be there for much of the summer, though of course I can ride home when I'm needed. I'm no more than two days out."

"To do what? Check my additions?"

He stirs his spoon around in his soup. As the master of his house, he has never been able to dictate what would be served him each night. "I wouldn't want you to be lonely."

"I've been thinking of teaching some of the younger slaves to read. There are several children in town with time on Sundays." Helen rings the bell for Mrs. Randolph.

"You'll get Miss Kingston to help you?"

"Mrs. Foushee now."

"You're getting a little old to be so much alone with them."

When Mrs. Randolph takes his bowl, the spoon clatters to the floor. She bends with a sigh to salvage it. She is hardly a discreet servant, but they have employed her long enough that they are stuck with her, as with a poor relation. "He won't even eat the soup with the first of the carrots," she says. "As sweet as I could make it and with a little cream too. You'd tell me if you were getting sick, sir?"

Asa nods.

128

"The man is just not one for soups," she says, backing out of the room with the bowl in one hand and the dripping spoon in the other.

"What would you have me do?" Helen asks. "Gossip with her all day? Sit in my room and write a novel?"

"I will say I'm happy enough you haven't found a husband yet. It's in my interest to still have a daughter to order around. Though you might find time to prepare for that day. Take a larger hand in the cooking, for instance." Mrs. Randolph has come in with two plates of fish, undoubtedly cold.

After she leaves, Helen smiles and accuses him of snobbery. He reaches across the table for her hand. "I wish I had a little trinket of yours to take with me to the capital. I would treasure it." He thinks of the portraitist who brought his small canvas and brushes to Long Ridge over a year ago. What has she been saving it for?

"I'll think of something," she says. "It must remind you of my virtues. I won't have you cursing the time I broke Mother's vase or remembering when Moll and I let the snake inside the house."

He ignores the fish and rubs her fingers between his. "You're always the home I want to return to."

That night, sitting at his desk next to the bed he used to share with his wife, he writes the president of the North Carolina Assembly to accept his assignment in the House of Commons. He is filling the seat of William Blount, who will serve as a delegate to the Continental Congress in Philadelphia. The path he's on is a ladder; men are being swept up the rungs to greatness. On a separate paper, he begins writing out instructions for his daughter: where the ledgers are stored (though she knows), the lists of negroes, the addresses of his purchasers, the coin available for new hatchets, shipping barrels, sugar.

The papers say the war is done, that the British surrendered at Yorktown in the fall. But still the ships are roaming the coast, as though the bitterness were not yet purged. Beaufort has survived the first seven years of war; the last few months will make no difference.

A pile of folded breeches lies beside Asa's dressing chair, where it has escaped the notice of all the women of the household. A hired man closes and ties the last trunk, stacking it on top of the others at the base of the front stairs. Two horses nudge heads. With their tails, they flick at the first of the summer flies. The session begins on April 13, and Asa sets out on a Wednesday, ten days before, to allow time for traveling the two hundred miles and then settling. He stands just past the carriage, looking out over the weedy grass and through the few scrub trees to the lip of the sea. It is a warm day, and he would be happy to shed his coat in the carriage except that he is now a North Carolina assemblyman. He will in all things be dignified. In the small traveling case that he will carry beside him, he has packed two quills and half a dozen new nibs that Helen bought for him in town. They have promised to write each other every few days, though he also imagines writing bills for the betterment of his state and soon his nation. He is newly concerned about his penmanship.

The night before, she gave him a soft package. He did not smile immediately upon opening it, so Helen rushed to explain. "I was making it as a fire screen, but I wanted you to have something to take, so it's now a pillow. It's supposed to be Long Ridge, but I've put in too many birds." He told her the embroidery was beautiful and thanked her. He said there couldn't be too many birds.

Through an open window, he hears a woman's yell; a few moments later, Moll rushes out the front door and down the stairs with his breeches in her hand. "You would've been pantsless, sir."

He motions to the coachman, who looks from Asa to Moll before coughing and reaching out for the stack of clothes. Moll knows it is beneath his station, but then so are most things they do. "I wish you safe travels," she says, and briefly bows her head. "May the Lord guide your horses."

Helen hurries from the house with a cloth-wrapped bundle. "Bread for the road," she says. Asa takes the warm package from her, and the two men stand there with full hands, uncertain of how to leave.

"I'll write you in the carriage," Asa says to his daughter.

"It will be illegible."

He presses her to his chest and then kisses her cheek. There are men who have no daughters, he thinks.

In trying to contain his emotion in the carriage, he misses the parting scenes of Beaufort: the dusty drive west out of Long Ridge, the street that divides the town from the ocean, the marshes that lead to pine forests that lead to hardwood. The roads are almost fully shaded before he can bring himself to look out the window as a man again, as a legislator.

That night Helen sleeps in her father's bed. She finds his shape in the mattress and lies next to it, resting her hand in the dip where his shoulder was. This is her tribute to him, but she doesn't miss him yet; she is too young to regret her independence. Through the open window, she can hear the distant chop of waves. Sometimes she thinks men are coming in rowboats, their oars splitting the water with that repetitive thwack. When she was younger, she had pictured them docking at Long Ridge, sneaking into the house, and carrying her away in a flurry of sheets. Before she could imagine where the boats would take her, she had always fallen asleep.

Now in the half-stages between consciousness and dreaming, she maps out scenes of reunion. She is sitting with her feet in the back creek when he appears; she is stirring cake batter; she is dozing in the gazebo. Most nights, she doesn't get to the point of having him speak. He is wearing a patched uniform with his musket strapped to his back, and they mostly just look at each other. Once she walked up to him and wrapped her arms around his chest and held him until she fell asleep. During the day, she remembers these figments as if they were real. When Mrs. Randolph asks her why she smiles, she has to stop herself from saying, "John

132

came home, and in his eyes I saw he loved me, and then I held him."

Tonight the sound of slapping water is the sound of John in a small boat. She places her dream-self on the edge of the bay, her bare feet in the water, and waits.

In the morning, three ships round the corner of the buffer islands and appear in Topsail Inlet. They slacken their sails just beyond the sandbars and reefs that protect the town from the sea. Helen watches them float, flagless, as she walks to town to purchase coffee. By the late morning, they haven't moved, and a small crowd of men has gathered by the docks to speculate. Their best guess is northern traders. One of the older oystermen calls to Helen when he sees her.

"Does your father have any shipments expected?" He knows Helen as he knows all the town's children, having none of his own.

She looks out at the three ships, resting her parcels against her hip. "We sent a load just before he left," she says, "and I don't think anything is wanted."

"They may be here for Johnson or Foot."

"I can go home to check the ledgers again," she says. "You don't think they might be British?"

"The British fleet is dead, miss, and there's certainly nothing in Beaufort for them."

"Looks like someone ought to pilot them in," a younger man says. "They must not have been here before."

"They're not fool enough to go rampaging around the shoals," the oysterman says. "I suppose they're waiting for rescue."

"Should we ask the rice men?" his companion says.

"Better send a boat out. They want to dock, or they wouldn't have come in at all. We can't get trade back soon enough."

Helen can make out the forms of men on deck, none of them moving quickly. Perhaps one is John, come for her after all, two years of fighting done and honorably released. She is tired, having woken up before dawn to walk the fields, policing the acres of pine. She sits on a stone bench on the slope between Front Street and the wharf and watches the fishermen ordering themselves. They decide to take out two dinghies, each with a pilot; a handful of men who have already brought in their nets take the empty seats from a mingled sense of duty and curiosity. There may well be a reward from the local merchant who's had his goods rescued. Surprise is what keeps men alive, Helen thinks.

She looks out at the phantom John, a speck on the ship. Is God offering her his hand? She is not superstitious, does not believe in graveyard ghosts, but if John truly was a passenger on one of those ships, wouldn't fate send her a dinghy? She has been seeing his face everywhere; it is only just that she should find it at last.

"May I come?"

The oysterman who first called Helen has the boat's rope half unwound. He used to let the children ride on his back when he was a younger man. He looks up at her with pleasure. "You wouldn't mind a short trip, miss?"

Did all explorers launch toward the unknown with such joy? She hoists up her packages and hurries down the slope, taking short steps to keep from stumbling. The oysterman reaches out for her burdens and she drops them in his lap, climbing in after. She has spent her entire life by the ocean and yet has never felt comfortable on boats. There is something additionally precious about the stability of land when surrounded by water, and this is what she loves about her home, not the water itself. The oysterman sits her on the thwart next to him and wraps his arm around her waist. He is happy to have secured himself a young lady.

"Are you scared of the open sound, miss?" In the breeze, his white beard tosses like puffs of cotton grass.

She smiles and shakes her head. "Not with you beside me."

In his role as gallant, the oysterman has avoided the hard work of rowing. The younger men in the boat take the oars and head south to the inlet where the ships are still and waiting. The sun hovers directly above them. Helen should've sent word to Mrs. Randolph so she wouldn't keep dinner waiting, but thoughtlessness is an adventure in itself. She buries her guilt beneath her fear of the ocean. The oysterman tells her stories of merhorses and Rahabs, and by the time they pull along the larger ships, her stomach is sore from laughing. A man throws a ladder down for them to climb, and the younger men go first to help guide the sailors to shore.

Helen is reaching for the rope when she hears shouts on deck.

She pauses, but there's nowhere for her to go. She is on a small boat in the sound with one hand on a rope ladder. The faces of two men appear over the side of the ship. After a brief look of confusion, they yell at her to board. She looks back at the oysterman, who is rubbing his hands across his shirt and shaking his head at her. Looking up again, she sees that one of the men is now pointing a musket at her. Where is John? Have they locked him up? The climb up the ladder is as undignified and brave an act as she has ever done, and she experiences it at the speed of syrup. The rope in her hands is bristly and warm, and the water that rocks up the side of the ship wets her ankles. Voices come at her from above and below. None of them are pleased. She is conscious of the wind sifting through her skirts, and the old man still left in the boat who will be able to see her legs. Halfway up, the fear blossoms into anticipation; if this is John's boat, John who was once a privateer, of course there would be men with guns. This is nothing but a theatrical gesture of his attachment. The hope lasts only a rung, and then she wishes she had brought pen and paper to bid her father farewell. She can read the name on the ship's prow, the *Peacock*, and decides this is not a dangerous name. At the very least, this is not a Spanish ship. The hull above water looks parched, stripped of paint. There are too many birds circling the ships, as though the sailors had been throwing out their bad meat, sure now of fresh provisions. They are still at war; of course. She reaches

136

one arm over the edge of the deck, and a young man in red offers her his hand. She accepts, as demurely as she would at a dance, and she is heaved on board and ushered at gunpoint to the main mast, where her companions are being tied hand and foot with ropes.

CHAPTER
FIVE

By all accounts, the war is over. The British lost at Yorktown in the fall. There have been skirmishes in the Caribbean, where it is still warm enough to spark men's blood, but on the continent the winter has cooled the armies' spirits. Only the Indians continue to fight. Generals are talking to generals, and accords are being drafted. King George's party has been replaced in Parliament, and everyone is for peace, from the mothers to the sons. The Americans are already looking hungrily westward. Grass is starting to grow over the graves of men who went to war and never returned.

In the General Assembly, Asa listens to the other representatives discuss plans for their districts: monuments, a local postal service, canals. Some are nervous about the loss of Britain's oversight and hope for a muscular constitution; others are glad to begin governance with no long history to cloud the country's logic. They will sit down and decide what must be true and leave out the rest, simple. Asa is lost in daydreams.

He has never had much to fear from a war. The worst danger he ever faced was as a boy, just sixteen; a fleet of Spanish privateers landed in Beaufort's harbor and spent a summer stealing boats and raiding the town.

For several years, the Spanish had been using Cape Lookout as a base to raid passing ships. The town built a magazine in case of attack and filled it with powder and shot. In the summer, boys at play took turns guarding it. But in 1747, after the Spanish had emptied the harbor of Beaufort's fishing fleet and come back again for its silver and the fresh meat from cattle and pigs that could not be gotten at sea, the magazine became necessary. As soon as it was necessary, it was captured.

Asa is old enough now to remember that summer only in patches. He must have been afraid, but he can only recall excitement. Major Ward, who was then very young and brave, called the soldiers and the farmers and the blacksmiths to arms; a hundred of them fought the Spanish back to their ships, killing a handful and, uncertain what to do with the bodies, burying them with some measure of respect in the town cemetery, for they were Christian after all. Afterward the governor gave them money to build a fort on Bogue Island, which they started and never finished, because there had been peace ever since.

Had Asa carried a gun? No, and though he's listened to the stories of men who shot at the rumps of the retreating Spanish, he hasn't felt the heft of a weapon in his own hand. Not when a weapon was needed, at least. He isn't jealous of those farmers who chased the Spanish pirates out of their harbor, nor does he wish to carry a gun in the current fight. He has chosen to build things, to piece together opportunities that jumble in the wake of wars, and to nurture a family that will outlast any glory of his own. He must have been afraid when the Spanish landed. But his father forbade him to join the farmers and his mother kept him away from the shore, so now he doesn't remember the fear. This is what parents do: shape the emotions that will color memory.

Now he is no longer a young man. His daughter is grown and wise, and she is entering a peaceful world. The legislators drone on. Asa takes pride in his role as public servant. He is pulling order from chaos, and when he returns to Beaufort, he will take credit for his daughter's fearless eyes. When he dies, she too will remember him as a faint but pleasant echo. He might even let her convince him of heaven. The war has ended, and the General Assembly is enjoying the warmth of April in Hillsborough.

But the British are not done fighting.

A courier arrives in the encampment at New Bern with a letter detailing the British treachery in Beaufort. Colonel Easton asks him how much time has passed, and the man looks at the star-speckled sky and says, "Some hours." The men are on their feet, pulling coats on and tying powder horns to musket straps. With an advance of cavalry and the rest scrambling horses and carts from the town, they will arrive in stages during the night. Easton tells them the British have blocked the port and prisoners have been taken. They will advance from the north and gather on the outskirts of town for orders. John understands that Easton is buying time. His own mind tumbles over itself. There are paths leading north and west from Long Ridge; Moll will know them, can take them to safety. Moll, who may or may not love her mistress. He has not seen Beaufort in nearly two years, years that have been lost to petty battles and days of marching. Since being stationed in New Bern, he has nightly imagined his escape, the road that would carry him south through the marshes to Beaufort and Helen. Two years have never passed so slowly. And now, when he and the army are on her very doorstep, she's in danger.

The night tunnels on. His borrowed horse is a plow-puller and sweats and heaves when asked to gallop. John slows him through the thicker forests, lets him drink at creeks, and then kicks him on the marshes, where he will pick up the scent of two dozen other panting horses. He has not had a letter from her since the fall, and then the writing was so small and cramped that he could not make out half the words. She told him endlessly of farming chores, of how the resin runs in warm weather and starts to thicken and halt with the frost. He skimmed the pages first, looking for softer words, before giving up and starting from the beginning, picking out the names of weeds and slaves. William Dennis may have been able to help, having had the same teacher guide his writing hand, but John could not appeal to his knowledge of Miss Kingston and the way she looped a long *S*. And yet the letter with instructions on sap farming is growing thin in his breast pocket and he has not begun to feel fear on his own behalf.

He can see the thinning trees on the outskirts of town. They make skeleton shapes in the blackness of midnight. Easton is standing beside his horse and a few men are pouring water from their canteens for their mounts, whose mouths are gray with foam. John's horse trembles, the muscles in his back shivering against John's legs. The men will first confirm that the town is still in American hands, and then spread out along the coastline to prevent the British from landing. The courier's letter said they had taken pilots, though of course the pilots could refuse to guide them in. John considers the fishermen he knows in Beaufort.

John asks for the eastern strip of coast. "Dennis is on that segment," Easton says. He asks to accompany him, and Easton tells him to sort it amongst themselves. The advance messenger returns with a report from the councilmen, who have gathered in the town hall and are drafting different versions of panic.

"The British are still on the ships, sir. They're in the inlet beyond Bird Island Shoal."

"The prisoners?"

The messenger looks at the piece of paper in his fist. "They haven't confirmed the names. For some of the wives, a man's absence isn't so odd, so none are willing to say one way or the other. At least two boats of fishermen. One said he saw a woman go with them."

"The British don't take female prisoners," Easton says.

"They wouldn't have known she was coming, sir."

* * *

John and William walk their horses into town, where windows are lit and faces shift behind curtains. The masts of the ships jut from the horizon like dead stalks, the sails wilting around them, breathing in the night wind. Even the gulls are quiet.

"She wouldn't have any reason to be by the docks," William says.

John rubs the reins in his hand. A few men, unarmed, have gathered on Front Street to watch the ships. The two soldiers turn left along the water and head for the turpentine plantation.

"Her father would have told the councilmen. They would already know she was missing. It must be one of the pilots' wives." William mounts his horse. "I'll ride ahead."

What can John do but let him go? His heart is yearning out of his chest, is as hungry for her as a magnet for its pole. His claim on her, unlike William's, is unspoken. They have promised nothing, and what else can feed affection? He sees her hands reaching, in the darkness of fear, for William Dennis. Her palm on his cheek, the tips of her fingers curling his hair.

John's horse stops by a clump of cordgrass. In the quiet just before dawn, the horse's teeth against the grass sound like an army marching. John sits on the curb of the road with the reins loose in his hand. Around him, the sky dips into a final blackness before the violet bleeds through. He is still sitting there when William Dennis rides up from the east, his knees digging into the side of his mount even after he has pulled it to a halt.

"There's no one at the house." The horse frets beneath him. "No one there."

"Did you find Moll?"

"Moll? There's no one at her house."

John climbs back on his horse and jerks its head toward the road. He rides to Mrs. Randolph's without telling William where he's going, without asking himself what her absence means. His only thought is for the time passing.

Mrs. Randolph hasn't seen her, will ask Moll, the father is traveling. The ships have not moved in the harbor. Two of her children are in the front room crying. Their hearth has only embers.

Mrs. Randolph is pressing bread into the soldiers' hands when they hear the musket fire from the shore. The men mount their horses outside but are stopped by another soldier riding north.

"They've snuck ashore in rowboats," he says. "We're pulling back to where we first gathered." Another round of shots.

"The prisoners?" William asks.

"On the ships, or dead. We're pulling back. They came in by the marsh just east of town. Wasn't a soul to stop them. Easton's calling for reinforcements from New Bern, though they couldn't get here till afternoon."

"So we're leaving the citizens without defense?" John should have been patrolling the eastern shore.

144

"They're not after folk here. Just the port. Cut supplies off to men inland. They've held Charles Town for two years, and they're not stringing ladies up." The man canters ahead and then wheels his horse around. "But they'll shoot us dead on sight."

In their first encampment, in the stand of skeletal pines just north of town, Easton has a map out on the ground. The penciled image of Beaufort — the order of the town grid surrounded by the undulations of bog and swamp and sound — is lit by a soldier's lantern. The colonel circles the town battery, a line of four six-pounder cannon pointing out to sea, and the magazine, which houses a barrel of powder and a few extra guns. Hardly worth a siege, but they are the only clear things that require defending. Easton guesses that the battery is already in British hands, so he orders six men to the magazine before the British find it, and another two men to ride to New Bern and ask for troops from the west. These games seem absurd when the British have mostly been vanquished. The most the colonel can do is prevent the next man's death. Easton warns his small militia, standing cold in the spring dawn, to study their own preservation. "We will bring the prisoners home," he says, "but we will not risk any blood beyond what's demanded."

Within the walls of the magazine, a brick house no larger than an outbuilding, John sits and studies the barrel of powder. It stands in a shadowed corner of the room. The men have boarded up the one window, so only a few slants of the day's light reach the floor. When John is not watching the barrel, he wonders why there

145

is a window at all in a powder magazine. It must have been a house first, a one-room house, the house of a bachelor. If Helen were in this room. But there are five other men, shuffling in the tight space, alternating between jovial rudeness and fear. The only softness in the room is the round keg, whose iron hoops curve like women's ribs.

A man standing at the boarded window says he can see British troops passing by outside. "Don't we shoot them?"

"We could just take these guns and powder back to camp," another says. "There's no worth in the house itself."

"If we left, we'd be surrendering."

"What about balls for the cannon? Aren't they aimed right at the ships?"

"Haven't any cannonballs. No funds for them."

"Not a man who could melt some iron scrap to make a ball?"

The men scuff their shoes along the wood floor and avoid each other's eyes.

"You don't think they'll kill us here?" William asks.

John presses his palms back against the cool brick wall. "I don't think they know this is a magazine," he says. From any angle, there is no room for heroism here.

After the British troops have passed, the world outside is once again silent. There is no indication that it's Friday in a fishing town, that they are three blocks from a wharf. That it's April, when children cannot be kept indoors. John pulls a biscuit from his bag. The other men watch and wait.

Helen has never spent so much time on a boat, even one that isn't moving. When the ship hugs the swells of the tide, her stomach rocks. Her eyes are tired from the sun and the salt, and her legs stagger beneath her like a child's. She has spent most of her time in the captain's cabin, which, with the removal of his maps and letters and gun, has been transformed into a lady's room. This token of respect has drained her of fear. When she considers her actions, her first thought is not God but John. And John's world is so much wider; her courage is expanding within it. Her chief concerns now are maintaining her digestion and impeding her town's capture. She has taken a vow of silence as her first act of rebellion.

When the second night falls, she seeks out the oysterman, who sleeps on deck with the other Beaufort men. A British soldier, no more than sixteen, watches them with his gun half-raised. The lantern tied to the main mast has been snuffed; they don't want to provide an easy target for the Beaufort cannon. She puts her hands on his wrists in the dark, feeling the rope against them. The British boy takes a step closer.

"There's little hope for rescue, miss," the oysterman says, scratching the ropes against his knee. "Not unless you can take this young fellow's gun and then maybe swim ashore. Are you much of a swimmer?"

Helen shakes her head.

"That's as God would have it. They won't harm you, miss. They haven't yet, have they? There, I knew they weren't so bad as all that. I won't say as there's great hope — you never know what makes sense to a man in wartime — but it does seem we're more prisoners for barter than for making a lesson of. It's too bad you don't know how to swim." He scrabbles in his beard with his tied hands and picks out crumbs from their supper.

The boy, having been patient, now motions Helen away with the tip of his gun.

An hour after Helen has fallen asleep in the captain's cabin, she is awakened by the rattling of the door. She crawls from the bed with soft feet and seizes a brass telescope that had been propped against the window. Standing behind the door, she holds the instrument above her shoulder, waiting, shivering. A man on the other side begins to moan; he slides his fists down the wood and begs for entrance. She can smell his fermented breath through the door.

"Go away," she whispers. She puts the telescope down. Her hands are shaking.

When the room is quiet, the man having either left or slumped into sleep, Helen pushes a trunk against the door and crawls into bed. She begins to plan. Her father would already have been alerted and would be approaching the town from the north with a regiment of Hillsborough legislators; they will arrive tomorrow evening perhaps. John would be here. John must be already here. They won't shoot the cannon and risk harming the prisoners. With her hands untied, then, she is the only one who can act.

Despite never having properly learned to swim, she is very good at treading water; she spent her childhood splashing in the shallows of the sound. If given several hours and frequent rests, she could probably swim to shore, or at least to Bogue Island, where someone would find her. But she could only do it if no one saw, if soldiers didn't line the decks to shoot her out of the water. Her second plan is to come upon a man unawares and take his gun. In her mind, this requires only a few quick movements, a twist of a wrist. Once she has one gun, she can convince the soldiers to give her more, as long as she comes upon them singly and with surprise. It will be a game, until she has gathered all the firearms on deck and the British are tied to the masts. The fishermen can then sail the boats to land and they will be free. Her third plan is to beg, like a woman. To take whatever her body affords her. To answer the man at the door, and use him.

She falls asleep before she is finished thinking.

The third and fourth days are no different; she is given bread and water and can move freely on deck. She does not speak to the British, some of whom give her fresh strawberries that they have stolen from the town's gardens. She eats them without a smile. She gives every man a look that suggests she would murder him if he touched her. The soldiers travel to shore in dinghies and return with prizes. Through the fishermen, who have no compunction about conversing with the enemy, Helen learns of Beaufort's state: the town is a new carcass, just unraveling, picked at by the British plunderers. Shots have been traded, but there are no men dead. In most houses, the fresh bread and meat were taken first, then men came back for the silver

— no worse than any bandits. The American regiments held their fire once the British threatened to burn the town. Some Beaufort men have locked themselves into the powder magazine, but the British have turned a blind eye to the villagers sneaking them food and drink, as though the humiliation of six men trapped in a single room was best ignored. Helen places John in all these settings: the front lines, the wounded, the magazine. Only after days without news of his body does she remember to pray.

On the sixth night, when the stars are out, she carries her chamber pot to the ship's side and empties it while a soldier looks the other way. She is grateful that she has been spared the indignity of the beakhead, where men sit on open holes above the ocean. But some convicts too are treated well before hanging. In her other hand she holds the telescope, just in case. She would use it on the stars, except that then she couldn't see a man behind her.

She returns to the captain's room and removes her stays and underskirts and shoes. She has saved her dinner and now wraps the boiled potatoes in a kerchief. The flask of water she ties with a cord around her waist. She climbs into bed and waits for the sounds of the ship to settle. First the hard sound of boots as the men patrol the deck. The laughter from the night's last mess. The creak of the capstans as the ropes are tightened. The splash of supper's refuse thrown overboard. Boat sounds, which she is now used to.

150

When she wakes, the wind is breathing through the door. She has a cramp where the flask dug into her side. She is cold, not having crawled beneath the blankets, so she wraps the captain's coat around her and puts the potatoes in its pocket. The sound of her door opening is swallowed by the general groaning of the ship. Without her shoes, she makes as much noise as a gull walking across the deck. Two boys are curled up near the quarterdeck, one with a musket in his arms. The Beaufort fishermen are tied and tangled together along the beam, some men resting their heads on others' stomachs. One is awake and leaning against the gunwale, stargazing or thinking about home. He glances at Helen as she walks by.

The ship floats in the channel behind Bird Island and Shark Shoal, the small dunes of sand and sea oats that buffer the town from storms. The prisoners have been shuffled to the third ship, the prow of which now faces Bogue Island and the ocean beyond. Helen can see the white sand glowing through the dark.

She does not think of sharks or merhorses when she climbs over the side of the ship and drops like a sack into the black water. She doesn't think of how she struggled to catch her breath racing Moll down the length of the creek. She clings to the sharp barnacled hull until she is sure the ship is silent, and then she sets out, one arm in front of the other, shivering in the cold water of early April, toward the glowing stroke of sand.

When she first stops to tread water, to rest her arms, she struggles to keep her head above the sea, which heaves around her like an animal. There are no waves, no surf, but a strong and terrifying heaving that swamps her mouth when she opens it. She starts to pull at the ocean, to yank it into her arms. Sometimes she can see the island and sometimes it disappears in the moving blackness. She finds herself facing the wrong direction and fights her body around until the sand appears again, surely closer now. She is infinitely heavy. Halfway to the island, she squirms out of the captain's coat and lets it sink beneath her. Her body buoys to the surface again, and for the next few yards she is hopeful, like a slim fish. She doesn't have enough strength to control the sound she makes in the water. Her splashing must be dampened by the night wind, for she hears no shots in the water.

She stops again and turns on her back to float, not caring which direction the ocean takes her. Her limbs are numb and melting. In the stars above she looks for patterns, but she cannot focus her eyes long enough to steady them. When the ocean rolls, so do the heavens. This is where her life has brought her, the life that she built so carefully from the blocks of duty and goodness. Love has killed her. If this is punishment, if God is looking down on her and witnessing her turned heart, then he will surely let her sink; the ocean is the space below the hand he pulls away, into which her body will drop. Her bones among fish bones, her beauty dissolved and consumed. She will learn whether or not her mother waits where the dead wait. She closes her eyes against the stars, waits for the hand to pull away. She waits. But still she floats. This is not what life has done to her, but what she, Helen, has done to her life.

Not a soul to witness. Not a soul needed. She begins to feel the water beneath not as a vast emptiness but as a vessel in which she travels. She cannot feel the cold anymore. A faith is resuscitated within her that is independent of her survival. The vessel moves whether or not she is inside.

Turning on her stomach again, she kicks out into the dark. She is choosing, and moving, and her will is God's will. The night carries her, and the next time she lifts her body up to gasp at air, her feet brush against sand. Her toes dig into the bottom, hungry for purchase, and she steps and crawls the rest of the way to Bogue Island, dragging eelgrass by her ankles.

She lies on the damp sand until her breathing steadies. The journey could not have taken more than half an hour, and yet she expects to see dawn soon. She wills her muscles to stop spasming, and gradually the shivers fade into a calm, bone-aching cold. She waits again for gunfire; nothing. Crawling on her hands and knees, she tops the nearest dune and digs into the gully on the other side. The sand still holds some of the day's warmth, and she rolls herself in it, coating her wet limbs in white grit. There is a wildness in this moment that she savors, beneath all her discomfort and fear. It is as if she had never been human. Layers of guilt and decency are scrubbed clean. She sleeps.

The gentle gray before morning wakes her, and she drags her stiff body inland, past another high dune, through blankets of pennywort and marsh elder, to the half-built fort. Its bundles of sticks resemble firewood piled high. She crawls around the side, through the unfinished wall, and curls up against the clay daub that coats the interior in patches. Through the open roof, clouds swell like dozens of bulbs. Her stomach begins to tighten, and she feels around her dress for the kerchief of potatoes. She finds nothing. They were in the coat pocket. She begins to cry, and the wildness collapses a little. The flask is still around her waist, so she drinks and falls asleep again. Her dreams are empty.

On Wednesday, April 10, a group of British soldiers walk from cannon to cannon along the town battery and drive barbed spikes into the vents so the artillery can't be fired. John hears the sound of hammering from the magazine, which has turned into a prison. Three men had managed to slip out one night, but a message was later sent from the colonel to maintain position. They periodically empty the night bucket when no soldiers are around, but the stench remains. There is no purpose in defending a barrel of powder in a siege. The British can just as easily set fire house by house; they have no stake in the powder. John would have slipped out too, except, as a poor man and an orphan, he cannot run the risk of discharge. There is no future for him without the honor of this position, and the future forms the bulk of his thoughts these days. He has to keep telling himself: Helen is either alive or dead, and these are unchangeable facts. Right now, she is either dead or she is alive.

A battering on the magazine door wakes John from his morning doze. A messenger from Colonel Easton reports that the British have retreated to the ships and are interested in negotiations.

"What sort of negotiations?" John asks. "They make the rules of this game."

"There were four British officers in New Bern prison," the messenger says. "They've been brought down for trade."

"Are all the prisoners safe?" William Dennis steps out into the morning and squints. A heavy sheet of clouds puffs out above them. "The woman?"

"We give and we get," he says, and orders them to report back to the encampment along the line of pines outside town. "Colonel wants the guns and powder too."

"Now he wants the powder," the third soldier says, and he and John heave it between them while William collects the dusty muskets and balls.

The British officers are already at camp, shackled and conversing with the American soldiers. They were treated well at New Bern, they say, especially by the ladies. This earns them a couple of slaps and some laughter. There is only danger when men forget they are men.

In the afternoon, a line of American soldiers waits by the wharf with the British prisoners in chains behind. A large row-boat approaches from the channel, carrying four dressed officers and six fishermen. When they pull up along the short pier, all guns are raised. Colonel Easton steps aside with one of the officers for a conference. John watches their hands, moving first with the stiffness of gentility and then with agitation. It is clear to everyone that there is no woman in the rowboat.

Easton orders the soldiers to step back. He nudges the British men forward, and William Dennis removes their chains while the fishermen are relieved of their ropes. The two parties shuffle past each other. No guns are lowered until the rowboat is halfway back to the channel and the anchored ships.

"They are keeping two pilots," Easton says, "to guide them out of the harbor. They will be released once the ships are in open water."

"They're leaving, then?"

"When they leave, they have promised to return the pilots."

"There was a woman," William says.

Easton takes a few steps away from the wharf, then turns back. He pulls his saber and digs the point of it into the boards of the pier. "They can't find the woman."

William looks at John, and John looks at his shoes, his head throbbing.

"There is a chance she escaped."

"No one saw?" One of the soldiers turns to look at the fishermen, who are still rubbing their wrists by the water.

"One man, who does not have a reputation for sobriety, says he saw her climb off the ship," Easton says.

"*Climb* off?"

"There is no reason to believe the British have harmed her. She may have escaped. They may send her back with the pilots. We cannot afford to make too many demands."

Some of the soldiers walk down to the water to hear the fishermen's stories of capture before Easton orders them back to camp. They do not understand what sort of a battle this is that has no end to it, where women can vanish like witches and there is nothing to defend. The two rivers that Beaufort sits between, the North and the Newport, have never made these men any richer. Easton has told them if the British take Beaufort, they will have New Bern and then the interior, but even the men who have not seen fighting know that this is a dying war. They are weary, homesick. The soldiers march back to camp in formation, their legs not reaching so high as they once did. The fishermen filter back to their homes, where wives are grateful and indignant.

Once the clouds drift away and the light begins to fade, the Beaufort regiment settles in for an evening of idleness. In a canvas tent, one soldier deals cards by candlelight. Two men stand beneath a pine and share a pipe. William lies on his cot with his hands covering his face. John walks into the woods. Un-followed, he continues into town. He sneaks into a merchant's house and buys bread and cheese and potatoes from the housewife, who is happy to be paid for the theft. At the wharf, he unties a skiff and with shallow strokes he rows into the channel, resting every minute, as if he were just a sculling pelican and not an American soldier.

The drunken fisherman, who could not have been drunk after six days of imprisonment, told John the woman had climbed off the prow of the third ship when it was pointing south, straight out to sea. Then she was drowned or beached somewhere, John said. The man had winked at him.

The channel is flanked by two scrubby sandbars that stand between Beaufort and the larger banks on the farther edge of the sound. John makes for Shark Shoal, the western patch of land. He pulls far enough along the bank to be out of range of the British ships, which are dark and still in the channel. It takes him half an hour to drag the skiff across the shoals. Even a small boat is not willingly pulled through wet sand. Every few steps, he whistles, but there is no reply. He scans the eastern and southern shores, but only fish skeletons interrupt the smoothness of sand. On the other side of the shoals, he can see the outlines of Bogue Island. If her body isn't there, he'll row across to Shackleford Banks, pick the sand apart, and then circle back to Bird Island. Then he will come home and in the morning begin again.

It is past midnight, and Helen is asleep. She holds in her hand a few stalks of half-eaten sea oats. She spent the day following the narrow shadow of the fort's wall as it moved around its circle, crouching in its shade. At noon, the sun inescapable, she had crawled out for sustenance. She dug up a clump of beach grass, cutting at the roots with her teeth, before she noticed the hulk of the British ships in the channel behind her. She crawled back to the fort and washed the sand out of her mouth with the remaining water in her flask. She saw phantoms crawling in the dunes. Tomorrow she will try to find her way home. After she sleeps.

When she wakes, it is still dark. Her mouth is hot with thirst. A dew has settled on her skirts, and a man is wrapped around her. His hands cross on her belly, and she feels them with her fingers.

Her scream comes out as a hoarse gasp. He reaches for her mouth to cover it, and when she is still, he runs his fingertips across her lips, once, and untangles himself. He crouches on the far side of the fort and waits for her to speak.

She cannot speak. There is a man whom she loves who is not her father, and God who carried her here is waiting to guide her out again, but she cannot recall an image of home to help him. God is crouching, waiting for her. There is not enough liquid in her to weep, so her eyes sting instead. The men will find her, take her, tie her up, and all she wants is home — not home: a coffer for her faith. She is not the one escaping; it is God who draws her on, who tells her that a little-practiced love is no love at all. He crouches there, too distant to touch, and asks her to spill her heart — that jar she carries, to let it soak into the unseen corners. Her lungs grow and brighten.

God uncaps a canteen and holds it out for her. She crawls to it and drinks.

Day arrives and the ships are firing on Beaufort. John feeds moistened bread to Helen, who wakes and sleeps.

He can see smoke to the north rising above the dune, beyond which the town is hidden. Small curls, not yet a conflagration. He rests her head on his coat and walks to the shore. An American sloop burns in the harbor. He doesn't know where she'll be safe, but the fort cannot keep them much longer. They need more water.

In the afternoon, she wakes from a nap and watches a sand-piper peck its way toward the fort, stopping to nuzzle in the ground or scratch its beak in its feathered side. When it sees her, it tilts its head and stays motionless.

"How do you feel?" John's voice sends the bird hopping and then fluttering out of view.

She turns toward him and cannot understand what is happening on this island. "When did you arrive?"

"In the night. You swam from the ship."

"I was here for a day, and you weren't here."

"I didn't know where you were."

He is sitting so far away from her. "My father?"

"We never knew that it was you. They sent word of the attack, but he can't come into the town. He thinks you're safe." A boom from the harbor makes her stand, but when the sun hits her face, she weaves and crumples to the ground again. John stays where he is. "We need to leave."

"You can't be here. Alone, with me," she says.

"I have a boat. We'll leave tonight, if the firing stops." He pulls a few small potatoes from his bag and holds them out to her on an open palm.

"My potatoes," she says. "You found them."

By dusk she is almost herself again. John's canteen is empty and only a heel of bread remains in his sack. They drag the boat back across the dune to the shore, where it will look no more formed than driftwood in this haze of light. They sit down on the sand in the boat's shadow and wait for the tide to lick up to them. She reaches for his hand. It's warm and dry, and she remembers for the first time his fingers on her mouth. She cannot bear the thought of leaving this island, the kindling fort. There is nothing she is not afraid of.

"You wrote so little," she says.

"You wrote of farming," he says.

She will go with him anywhere.

He places her palm on his chest until her breathing matches his. The last tinge of gold in the sky evaporates, and the spindles of smoke from town now blend into the darkness.

They launch the boat, row around the back of the sleeping British ships to Bird Island Shoal, pull the boat across sand, and row to the far edge of town, east of the wharf, where they drag the boat into the marshes at the base of Long Ridge. The journey has taken several hours, and when they make it to the main house, up the stairs, and through the door that William Dennis had forced open, Helen falls to the floor of the hall.

John lifts her and she tells him to go away. He searches the house until he finds a bedroom that faces the sea. He lays her down gently and waits. Her eyes are closed. He reaches to take off her shoes, but she has none. The bottoms of her stockings are shredded and dark with mud. He cannot take off a woman's stockings. She tells him to go away. She puts out her hand into the darkness. He takes it in both of his, as if it were all of her. He kisses it. She sits up and reaches out her other hand and when he moves closer she wraps it around his neck. She finds his mouth and holds it in hers and will not let it go.

When he lowers her body back to bed and rubs his thumb across her cheekbone, she reminds him to come back for her. He has been missing from his regiment for two nights and a day, and if they whip him for desertion, then he will be back very soon. She smiles and he folds the blanket over her.

On his way back to camp, he stops at the neighboring slave cabins on Cogdell's land. A man sits on one of the porches, eating a slice of white cake. He is shirtless, and from the man's lantern John can see the glistening of blood on his back. A needless guilt washes over him. John asks for Moses's cabin, and the man points down the row.

He knocks quietly. After a few moments, Moll cracks the door. Seeing John, she sidles out and closes the door behind her. She motions toward the rice field behind the cabins, and they begin to walk. "You found her?" she asks.

"She's back at Long Ridge. Can you stop in to see her?"

"I'll go in the morning. There's no work now; we've all been waiting."

162

"There was a man beaten." He turns to look down the row of cabins at the single light on the porch.

"Tried to run away. Went north instead of south, ran right into the soldiers' camp. They try to hold on to what order is left." Her arms are crossed against her chest. "Aunt Caty stole him some dessert from the kitchen." As they shift their feet in the hard dirt between the cabins and the sunken rice furrows, a chorus of tree frogs erupts nearby. "You better go. I'll look in on her."

He puts his hand on her shoulder and thanks her.

"I'm almost sorry you two didn't run off after all. I think it might've been just the thing for her."

"It seems this town won't let people go," he says. He walks her back to her cabin. When he passes the man on the porch, John nods. The man has finished the cake and is licking his fingers.

In camp again, he slides onto his cot next to William Dennis, whose eyelids flicker. He could have told them she was dead. He could have asked her to marry him. They could have rowed to Wilmington. He presses his lips together and remembers as he falls asleep.

On Friday, April 12, Colonel Easton receives a letter from Governor Burke, warning him that three ships carrying two hundred and fifty British soldiers were sailing to Beaufort after being told the town possessed a large quantity of military supplies for the Continental Army. There is some confusion when one of the captains calls out to the men, "Three more ships coming!" but the letter is clearly dated April 3, and has simply arrived too late. With the extent of Beaufort's military supplies covered by a single tarpaulin in this makeshift camp, Easton feels some of the sting of irony. He ignores John's reappearance, and when William Dennis tells him John fetched the woman prisoner back, he chooses to believe him. Two other soldiers have already vanished without any likelihood of return. It is hard for a colonel to keep his men camped out in a field at the far edge of a siege.

The cannon fire continues on Saturday through a slow rain. On Sunday, Easton and his captains gather in the home of Mr. Foushee to meet with the town councilmen. Mrs. Foushee, the former Miss Kingston, pulls John aside to help her arrange meat tarts on a tray.

"She's doing well," Mrs. Foushee says, plucking the little pies from a basket on the sideboard. "Would you taste one? Here. She's had a few sneezes, but nothing for concern. Won't tell me what happened, only that she swam for shore and you rescued her."

"Her father's been told of her safety?"

"Do they need more salt? I could sprinkle some over. Yes, and she's got a letter from him too. He's in New Bern, waiting for them to let in townsfolk. You needn't finish it — here, you must be worn and worried. She thinks very highly of you, I can say that. Go sit with the men. I merely wanted to meet you proper. And to thank you."

He carries a tray back with him and passes it among the soldiers. Men are discussing options, both for victory and surrender, and any details are obscured by

164

the language of pride. It is a wounding thing to live under siege. John cannot follow the conversation. He leans into the corner of the room, resting his shoulders against the walls, the back of his head grateful for support. He can no longer allow time to carry him, can no longer avoid making decisions, or circumvent his affections. His happiness is now dependent. When his mind is at rest, it rests on her. The room, crowded with regiment men and merchants, captains and fishermen, only reminds him of her stillness, her damp hand in his, the stockings in disarray. Their voices melt to her voice, hoarse. The conversation surges, heads shake, and he sees her limbs trembling in the darkened fort. There is soft applause and a general pressing of hands, and some of the faces are smiling. Will he have to present himself to her father? What material hopes can he possibly offer in wartime? Another cousin of his has a home here, and no heirs, but those are his only prospects. Easton is scribbling instructions on paper and the soldiers are standing, stretching, arranging for their exit. He could still die in this battle, and she would be alone again. Mrs. Foushee squeezes his elbow and smiles at him as he falls into the line of leaving men. They are outside again, and the evening is cool from the rains. She will be by herself tonight in a large house; even his legs ache for her.

At camp, William Dennis says, "Now aren't you glad we saved that powder?"

Helen sleeps late on Sunday, for there is no one to wake her. When she puts her feet on the floorboards, their groan is the first sound she hears, the first mark of a human on the house's emptiness. She is hungry, but Mrs. Randolph is feeding her own children on the other side of town. Moll is feeding her husband. Some tavern keeper must be feeding Asa. There are no biscuits in the pantry. In the back garden, the chickens are roosting in shrubs; no one has cooped them, and if she counts, she is sure to find one missing. Still in her stocking feet, she hunts for eggs, scrabbling in the bushes and behind fence posts until she finds two, brown and spotted. She stirs them in a pan with butter and onion and fries them over the fire.

She puts on clean stays and a skirt. After staying in bed for two days and being fussed at by the women who visited, she is ready to carry herself again. She takes a pencil and paper to the pine acres and makes note of the troughs that need replacing, the bark that needs to be whiskered, the weeds that should be cut. The catface trees have been neglected. The barrels of turpentine in the mill that were ready for shipment have been emptied by the British. When the ships leave and the slaves return, she will have them work double time to replace the lost inventory.

She doesn't remember that it's Sunday until almost noon. She walks to Cogdell's cabin, but its benches are empty and she sits at the altar alone. A skink lazes on the windowsill, and when she reaches out for it, it takes a few sluggish steps and then stops. Its skin is soft and papery, and its chest moves in and out beneath her fingers. She kneels down to find its eyes. They are black and deep and mirrored; she can see her own face in them. No slaves are looking for God today.

Everyone she passes on the walk into town is quiet and watchful. The masts of the three ships in the channel cast long shadows. The church near the wharf has lost the corner of its roof to a cannonball, and Helen must step over a pile of rubble to enter the nave. A woman and a man sit inside on opposite sides of the aisle. Helen sits next to the man, who is raking his beard. He smiles when he sees her.

"How'd your fleeing go?" he asks.

"I suppose I should've waited a few hours, then. I'm glad to see you."

The oysterman pats her knee. "We're all taken sometime or another. I was ready for them to take me, and I'm pleased to be let go. I don't try to hold on to my life too dear."

"Your wife must have missed you," she says.

"And who's to say they won't come for her tomorrow?"

Their whispers echo off the walls of the church, and the other woman has turned around to frown at them. Helen leans closer to the old man's ear. "I thought I couldn't swim, but the ocean carried me right to Bogue Island, just as you said. In the end, I wasn't afraid. And then a soldier came for me and brought me home."

"Next morning they rowed us to shore and took our ropes off and handed us right over. Five days of my life I didn't need to wake by dawn or work in the oyster banks. And you're right, she was glad to have me back and showed it too."

"Then what do we ever worry about?"

The woman in the front pew, who had been praying for her son, stands and walks out of the church.

On Monday night, the men who have been collecting lumber gather to lash the boards together and paint them with pitch. They work in darkness on the grassy lawn of Long Ridge that slopes down to the water. They are mostly hidden from the British here. Helen has given them space and some raw pitch and now brings them mugs of drinking chocolate. The townspeople work on one raft, and the soldiers construct another. She avoids giving a mug to John because she is nervous of him, so she speaks to William Dennis instead, whose hands get tangled in the ropes; by the time she moves on, he has several splinters in his hands. The women gather in clusters by the front stairs.

Six men carry each raft on their shoulders. Their procession along Front Street down to the wharf resembles two moving altars and a train of congregants. On the pier, John and William tie the single barrel of powder to one end of a raft and unwrap the long fuse. The men slowly lower the rafts into the shallow water, where their presence changes the sound of the waves. The town waits for a few minutes, but the ships remain dark and quiet. The tide is slipping out, tugging at the bundles of scrap wood. There is only a sliver of moon to see by until they light the first torch.

The fire moves slowly into the pitch, simmering. The men shove the rafts into the harbor, and the wind tugs the fire up. Men and women move back from the shoreline. The tide is patient, and the rafts bob on the water. In a few minutes, tiny lights appear on the ship decks. A few shouts carry over the harbor. The rafts are halfway there, blazing now, a spectacle of light that reveals neighbors' faces.

Without a chaperone, Helen finds John and takes his hand and kisses its palm. She slips a small wrapped parcel into the pocket of his coat and fades back into the crowd again. He has trouble breathing.

They can hear the winches pulling the British anchors up when the barrel explodes in a spasm of sound and light, sending shards of burning wood into the water and in arcs onto the sandbars, where they burn and pop and set skinny trails of fire running through the lines of grass.

In all the noise, the town is silent, watching, taking whatever evidence they can of God's husbandry.

The rafts become mired in the marshes by Bird Island Shoal, where the fires burn through the pitch until they reach wet wood; the remnants crack and sigh until the blaze dies out. The smoke coils for hours after.

In the morning, the three ships are gone, and the two remaining pilots row to Beaufort in a dinghy, glad not to have been burned to death.

Long Ridge looks unkempt, and Asa has only been gone ten days. He spent one afternoon in the assembly hall of Hillsborough, surrounded by other wise and landed men, before the news reached him and he turned to panic. He told the others his plantation was in danger, the home he had built to stand taller than the others, his rich acres of pine. But all he could think of was his daughter, Helen as an infant screaming, Helen as a child in her first blue gown, as a domestic tyrant, with chicken pox, with Moll, on Christmas, the almond cake she made for his birthday, the painted portrait he's never seen, her kisses until she became too old to kiss. There was a woman taken prisoner, Easton said, and Asa knew it was his.

His memories of the Spanish privateers, his offhandedness, must have brought this cruel repetition. Except unlike him as a boy under siege, she was alone. She had no parents to tell her to stay back, to worry not. He abandoned her, and someone else saved her.

There are black streaks of pitch on the grass, and sand has been tracked up the front stairs. Inside, his daughter is unchanged. She is so thin, her face is browned from sun, her feet are bare, and she is just the same. He holds her and he kisses her forehead, and she lets him. They sit in the parlor and he won't let go of her arm.

"They were gentlemen, really," she says. "I had no trouble."

"It was God watched over you."

"I suppose it was."

"God was the father to you when I was gone." He is recalling all his words spoken against his daughter's faith. "I should sponsor the rebuilding of the church."

"I'm glad you're home again. Tell me what it was like."

He stands up to get his satchel, to show her the papers he's been working on, but as soon as he leaves her side, his fear returns. He sits down again. "I am used in a way that I am not used here," he says. "I'm working not just for us, but for everyone, it seems. What will be a nation. Of course it means everything that you're here to keep the business steady."

"You're going back, then?"

"The British won't return," he says. "They're already drafting treaties in Philadelphia. You needn't be afraid."

"I'm not afraid," she says, rising from the sofa and breaking the grasp her father has on her arm. She pours him a glass of Madeira wine. When someone knocks on the front door, Asa spills a little of it in his lap. "I can't stay on this land forever," she says.

"There's someone at the door."

"Have you thought what might happen when I marry?"

"That's a long way off."

"I've done what I can here. I've managed the pines and taught as many slaves as were willing to listen. You're no longer here to take care of."

"You need someone to take care of?"

"Myself, mostly."

There is another rapping at the door.

"Please, dear," he says.

When she returns to the parlor, John is with her, his hat in his hand. Someone has cleaned his uniform, or he has borrowed the clothes of a fellow soldier. He still smells like smoke from the rafts. Asa rises to take his hand. "I hear I must offer you my gratitude."

"I merely assisted a fugitive," John says, looking at Helen for some sort of confirmation.

171

Before the men are seated, Helen tells her father she's in love.

Asa feels weak, his stomach tender. After her rejection of William Dennis, he had moved past frustration into a kind of security. So she wouldn't marry, some women don't. All the better. He had refashioned his life around her intransigence, and now he needs her. He doesn't hear John ask his blessing, though he cannot take his eyes off the soldier's face. "Who are you?" he asks. "You think you'll marry in my house? Who are your people?" He should be standing for this, but he can't trust his legs.

"There's little I can offer that you would value, sir." John would rather fight another war than ask a man for his daughter.

"You won't have this land, if that's what you're after. You won't get anything through her." He looks at Helen again. "When was all this happening?" He is betrayed.

She reaches for his stooped shoulder but he shakes her off.

"This is not to be discussed. You will leave us now, sir. I am recently returned from Hillsborough, and I would like to rest in my home with my child." He is certain he is going to vomit.

Helen goes to stand by John.

His empire is crumbling. He tries to recall his own young love, the bride he brought home to this lonely farm. Her shy face, her shy feet. She would not let him see her unclothed. When he was finally allowed into the birthing room to witness Helen — the third child, the one who survived — his wife was raw and bare. He was shocked, and then she was carried away as gently as she came to him. A woman stripped to her essence and evaporated. This was not Helen. He would not have a man see her like that. He would not have her loved, and certainly not lost.

"No," he says, and again, louder. "Get out of this house." He stands and takes his daughter's arm, supporting himself as much as stopping her. John begins to back toward the door. "This is over. This home is complete. God has blessed us as we are." John is out the door and down the stairs, and Asa still calls after him from the porch, Helen at his side. "Don't return here, to my home. You are the son of no one, and you will not be mine."

His voice begins to break, and Helen guides him inside. She sits him in a chair by the north window that looks out to the acres and hands him another glass of Madeira. Asa is surprised to see her face dry and composed. She kneels at his feet.

"Long Ridge is ours," he says. "Not a poor soldier's, not a privateer's. He has no loyalties. You think he'd love you? He'd sell you to the Cherokees. He'd trade Long Ridge for a sloop of his own." The more he says, the more he hears his words dropping like coins into an empty well. "Your mother would be ashamed." Her face does not change. "I should've married you off at sixteen with Moll. You know she's now with child? I don't want to look at you anymore. No, stay. Stay." He puts a hand on her hair. "I can sometimes see your mother in you. Somewhere in you is her gentleness." He smiles. "Darling. In the fall you had your picture made. Don't look surprised — I knew the painter was here. What was it, a miniature? You must have been saving it for my birthday. Give it to me now, so that we may make up. I never had a portrait of your mother."

"I don't have it."

His hand moves onto her cheek, smooths over its smoothness. "I don't mean to be angry with you."

"I made it for someone else."

He puts his hand back in his lap. There is a stain from the spilled Madeira. He must give his pants to Mrs. Randolph as soon as she returns. Where was she, while Helen was falling in love?

"I gave it away."

"Tell me what it looked like." It is only the afternoon, and he is thinking already of sleep, of what a night's sleep could do for him. He has lost his energy for fighting now; he could do it better in the morning.

"It was just a little thing. My face, my hair. It wasn't a very good likeness."

"Tell me about it."

Past him through the window, she can see the distant catface trees.

A few days later, trading ships begin returning to the Beaufort harbor. Asa promises funds to the priest for the church's rebuilding. Children collect the British cannonballs and sell them back to the regiment, which is in the process of disbanding. There is no other place to send the soldiers. The day before Asa leaves again for Hillsborough, Helen packs his trunk and makes supper with the guidance of Mrs. Randolph. She scoops out

174

hard rolls, fills them with oysters and sauce, and lays them on cabbage leaves. She bakes him an apple for dessert. When he is asleep and dreaming, she packs her own bag: a coat, her letter from John, a license for their marriage.

In the morning, a Barbadian ship sails out of the harbor through the channel between the shoals, past Bogue Island and Shackleford Banks, into the Atlantic. She is gone.

Part Three

1793–1794

CHAPTER
SIX

After they bury the barrel in the churchyard, with the curate reading the liturgy and the words of rest, they do not speak to each other. John returns to the empty house, the upstairs window still open, and Asa walks back to Long Ridge. October's warm spell is ending. Asa lights a fire in the parlor and lies down on his side on the sofa, folding his arms tight to his chest, hands clasped together, in a position almost like penitence. With his eyes closed, he pictures Tabitha. His only grandchild, the last in a line of women. Her body cramped inside a keg, wet, preserved. He had asked to shift her to a coffin, but John refused. Perhaps he wanted to think of her body as indissoluble. Both men were tired; there was little argument.

Nor was there any victory to claim. Asa swore the child would die if taken, and the child died, and what does that mean? Nothing. We are all dying.

He may be angrier tomorrow. Now he can only search vainly for sleep. When the fire dies out, he is still awake. He could get a blanket, but that would be an indulgence. He pulls his hands up to his mouth and blows into his cupped palms. His breath warms his face, like the breath of a child.

Mrs. Randolph wakes Asa when she comes to cook his breakfast. They are both slower now. When she bends down to sweep the ashes out of the fireplace, he tells her please don't, he can do it when he rises. She nods and waits, kneeling on the flagstones for a few moments before standing again. Her children are older now, a few of them married, and he has repeatedly asked her to move to Long Ridge. She likes her independence, but then Asa has never been as alone as he is now.

"You should have the young man live here," she says. He doesn't answer, so she climbs down to the cellar to pull scallions and strips of pork. The stock has shrunk since Helen's death, and half of the shelves now stand empty. Mrs. Randolph looks at the jars of sugar and cocoa and doesn't know what he'll need them for, now that Tabitha won't stop by for sweets. If only there were another woman to come and see him. Pity Widow Dennis had passed on; there might have been a match. She resolves to adjust his purchasing. It's hard to keep a ready kitchen for a single man. She'll have to stop in on John now too — make sure he's feeding himself and keeping the rats out. It's pride that keeps them apart, gives her twice the work.

Asa decides not to get up from the sofa. Who is watching to see him take his place at the head of an empty table? Mrs. Randolph finds a tray for his plate, and he watches the food until all the warmth is gone and Mrs. Randolph has left the house to forage in the garden, and then he touches it with his fingers. The

180

porridge has begun to harden. He scoops into it with his hand and brings it to his mouth, eating as cleanly as he can. He dips his fingers into the mug of cider she brought, then licks the taste off. If he were a blind man, he would have no images to haunt him. He sleeps again.

Mrs. Randolph finds a blanket to cover him. She sweeps out the ashes.

Every corner in John's house is a corner she once rounded. The walls still carry her fingerprints. When the wind comes through the bottom of a propped window, it makes the same sound as when Tab was in the room, and John keeps turning to find her. She does not even visit his dreams, which he spends haunted, hunting her, calling her name down empty paths, standing up in a skiff to look for her head in the waves. Waking, he feels like a plug has been pulled from the bottom of his feet, and all the unnameable things have drained out of him. Touching a doorknob, lifting a fork, he fears that the husk of him will break. This was a house the two of them came to, and is not a house that holds just one.

He drags his mattress down the road to the store, pulling a ridge of dirt behind him, and settles it in the back room, where her presence is most faint. He sleeps there for three days before he can open the store again. The only things to eat are candy and dried fruits, and he gorges on these, finding her in the sweetness. The first customers discover a rattled, ransacked space. He sells his goods without speaking, though he gains nothing from silence. He sometimes wishes Asa would stop by, or even Blue Francis, so he could grab a man's shirtsleeve and say, "Do you remember when? And the way her eyes fit in her face?" They would look down at their hands and speak of her shell-pink fingernails. He is grateful that Asa does not visit, or Blue Francis, who hardly knew her.

A boy comes in one afternoon with eggs to sell. John considers him from across the counter: his nubby hair, his wide brown eyes, his little straw basket.

"Only five eggs here," John says.

"That's what I got," the boy says.

"Who's going to buy five eggs?"

"To put in a pie, or any other thing."

"They'd only last a day."

"Then it's a day's worth of eggs."

John counts out a quarter dollar in coins. The boy counts them again. "You're taking that money back to your mother?" John asks.

"They're my chickens."

"And what'll you spend it on?"

"You have any peel?"

"Lemon or orange?" John asks, before remembering he has neither. The night before, after the town had guttered into darkness, he had sat on his mattress in the windowless room and eaten all the candied peels, their sheen absorbing the only vestiges of light in the air. They flickered in his hands. When they were gone, another thing that reminded him of Tab was gone, and he slept again.

"Orange, please," the boy says.

182

"Save your money for something nicer. Moll won't like you spending it on candy."

The boy kicks the counter. John never got to know Moll's son, though they came into the store sometimes. He was born after John took Helen to sea, and when they returned they had their own pregnancy to tend. Without Helen, John had trouble facing Moll. He bore a guilt that all men bear who lose their wives in childbirth; the sight of other women embarrassed him.

But here is a boy who is eleven, maybe twelve, who could have died also, or instead.

John watches him move idly around the store, brushing his fingers against the things he could buy for a quarter dollar. When the boy stops to inspect something, he rises up on his toes, bouncing his ankles. John cannot imagine the energy it takes to achieve this. If he stays here alone for another week, he will lose the ability to move at all. He will close his eyes and grow into the ground and a rough hide will cover him. He closes his eyes to test the feeling. There is a quiet in his limbs that is very soft and easy, and he almost can't breathe out of fear of himself.

A button hits his forehead. He opens his eyes. The boy is tucked behind a stand of brooms, smiling.

He is just a child. Has lost nothing.

"What's your name again?"

"Davy."

"Would you like a job? I'll be needing some help. Stocking, seeing to customers."

"Putting in orders?"

John leans his arms onto the counter and looks at the boy intently. "You can leave that to me."

"Just that you seem to be out of things, like peel."

The receipts on Asa's desk are out of order. He hasn't entered them in his ledger since John left with Tabitha, but the mail has not ceased, and business piles up. His turpentine production slowed after the war, after Helen was gone, and now he can see even less incentive to labor. The empire he had mapped for himself is shrinking. Cogdell, his neighbor to the west, has put in an offer for a third of Asa's pine acres, perhaps to start farming tobacco. Asa cannot find a reason to refuse. His hands are sieves. His body is losing its cohesion, like old paper gone to dust. The line of Asa's blood has reached its terminus. He has stopped imagining a future, the way he did when he was young and every path led to better versions of his own life. Paths narrow and end; his legs are weary.

He wants to ask John to dinner, to ask John to live with him. Long Ridge wasn't built to house one old man. But when he pushes aside the receipts and the unopened letters and draws a blank page toward him, he is frozen. The invitation cannot be written. This is a man who has, in selfishness, taken away everything Asa has loved. His daughter, his granddaughter. Both seaborne and now dead. He is perhaps most frustrated at the obliqueness of John's guilt. Women die in childbirth. (But Helen may not have married at all, that was always a possibility. Would he have given up the chance at Tab to keep Helen? Would he have sacrificed

184

Helen to have his own wife back, whole? There is a reason men do not decide their own fates.) Yellow fever is capricious. If Tab was going to die, she would have died on land or at sea. (But he stole Asa's chance to be with her at the last, to minister to her soul. Where is her soul now without religion's stamp?) His thoughts are all circular, leading him back to self-blame as much as to hatred of his son-in-law. The endlessly forking paths of his youth have become an inescapable loop. Death is a given; then where is his death? He can only conclude that God has spared him to suffer.

There are too many crosses to bear and still proceed; they have collapsed him. He is laid out, waiting for his body's end, his joints screaming under the weight of the crosses on his back. He does not have the strength to contemplate forgiveness. He dips the quill in ink and asks John to dinner.

She had loved the first child because she had no choice. It came out of Moll's body still attached and its dependence bred devotion. She loved before she could stop herself, before she knew any better.

Two years passed before her second child, and by then she understood that these babies belonged to somebody else. Love was weakness. Love was acknowledging the rightness of the world, and this she could not do. The children were beautiful and they deserved affection and she would do her almighty best, but her firstborn son was the last thing she allowed herself to cherish.

She wonders if her own parents, whoever they were, felt this. If the farm in Virginia, which she only remembers as swatches of green and hard labor, broke them of any love. Did they run away? Were they beaten to death? Does it make a difference?

She crawls next to Moses on the mattress but does not touch him. Davy sits in the corner and rocks the baby in its wooden cradle.

Moses speaks quietly. "Why don't you take her to the fields?"

"It's dangerous. There are snakes."

"The other women take their babies."

"Some do."

"Those who want to feed them from the breast."

"I didn't take the others."

"You took Davy."

She did take Davy. She had woken up in astonishment each morning to find him beside her. His fists like flower buds. Even when he was older and the other children went to the granny, she hoisted him on her back, singing to him in the rows, or tying him in a sling from a branch when she was tired. His smile, his little pearl teeth, did not belong to the plantation, or Cogdell, or Moll. Not even God owned him.

But the love he demanded of her was finite. She had just one jar of it, and when she gave it to him, she had none left.

When the second child arrived, Moll's eyes were clear. She saw it for what it was: a burden, a weight tied to her ankle, a reminder of their mutual fate. A victim.

If she had understood this sooner, she may not have loved her son.

The new baby is nothing but another body. This is what she tells herself to survive.

"She'll live," she says to her husband.

John is pulling down all the packages of cotton and string and foolscap from the shelves in the store's back room when Davy finds him. His mattress, tangled with a damp sheet, is littered with parcels. John steps among them clumsily, and when he trips on a small box and falls to his knees, he begins to punch his fist against the soft bed.

"I came for work," Davy says, standing in the doorway. "You looking for something?"

John stays bent among the parcels, so Davy retreats to the store. A young woman is fingering some raw wool and looks at Davy with concern. He is not old enough for much pride, so he smiles at her and opens his hands wide the way he has seen shopkeepers do. He is too nervous to form any phrases. He stands still with his hands spread and hopes she understands his role in this business.

"I'd like a little of the wool," she says, and a surge of ownership rises in Davy and warms him.

He pulls the skeins she asks for and carries them to the counter. He stands there for a moment, assessing the goods, his ease in handling them, when he remembers he should be on the other side of the counter. With a loud cough, he masks his misstep, hurrying around to the back. He takes the money she gives him because he doesn't know the price of the wool and in her face he cannot detect any deceit, and deceit is an expression on which he was raised. When he thanks her for the coins, he looks straight in her eyes and dares her to punish him. She takes the wool with a smile — she is almost still a girl — and leaves him alone in the shop, a master at last.

John comes out of the back room to find Davy rearranging the jars of spices, in order from dark cloves to the brightness of ground ginger. The mace, fire-bitten, sits on the shelf alone, uncategorized. John picks it up, and it's a comfort. The boy's organization touches him. He wants to remember Helen, her line of ship treasures arranged by size and with such affection, his body wrapped around hers, but he has a greater hurt that needs honoring. He cannot keep all of his memories and survive.

"I should have an apron," Davy says. "They might not guess I'm a shop man. Also, you need more colorful things, or folks won't stop in to purchase. And baskets. My mother is always wanting a good basket, for they break and fray all the time."

"Do you know where my house is?" John asks.

"I suppose so."

"In the hearth room, on one of the shelves, there should be a parcel in brown paper."

"A box?"

"Thin and soft. Would you look for it?"

"Just walk in? No one around?"

John sets the small jar of mace on top of the ginger. Would it have been easier to lose a son? There is something unprotectable about a boy. The journey he makes, to life or death, is simply the one he forges. But Tab — and Helen — lay in stillness, in wait, breath held, for the world to wreak its vengeance. He should have served them better. It is his fault. His own fault. He scrambles to climb out of that thought. He is getting better at dipping in and out of the darkness. In these moments of paralysis, what carries him up again is the reassurance that there is no grief left to him. There is no further sorrow. He has been to the bottom of it and seen God's worst. A man who loses his daughter to the world is his own punishment. He forgets what his daughter actually was, how her eyes jumped at the unknown, how she sought herself in isolation and dreamed her own hand into battles.

Davy is cautious of getting beaten, so he insists on an apron before walking to John's house. He meets the eyes of the men he passes and feels golden in his white smock. The door is unlatched, and when he sticks his head in, he sees a woman's figure on the floor of the hall, scrubbing the pine boards in idle circles, no more deliberate than a crab sifting through sand with one claw. He recognizes the wild white-and-drab frizzles of Mrs. Randolph's hair. She must have been loaned out from the big house at Long Ridge. She once brought bread to his mother when she was too laid up to bake. Moll was proud and wouldn't eat it, so Davy didn't tell her that the white woman's bread was better. It must have had a little sugar in it.

The boy doesn't know how to address the older woman, so he whistles. She starts up, sending a splatter of dirty wash water across the wall. He can see the panic in her eyes before she remembers.

"Is that Moll's boy? What are you doing?"

"I work at the store now," he says, coming inside and shutting the door behind him as if he owned the door and its hinges and its rusted iron latch. "I need to find a parcel for Master John."

"Master John, is it now? Go on, you seem to know what you're about, but no snatching from the pantry."

"I *work* at the store," he says again, sidling past her with some disdain.

The hearth room is shambled with boxes and jars and loose paper and dust. It looks as if an October storm has blown through and no one has set it to rights. Davy picks up a few of the smaller boxes and stacks them in a corner on top of a wooden trunk. They leave behind empty mirrors of themselves in the dust, ghost outlines. He begs a whisk broom from Mrs. Randolph and sweeps the dust around, fetching it from underneath chair legs and pushing it in circles until it has collected itself, the particles finding one another like family. He opens the back door and sweeps his pile out in dramatic bursts, each accompanied by a muffled howl of pleasure. The floor ready now for Mrs. Randolph's wet rag, Davy turns to the shelves, righting glass jars, refilling them with spilled beads, metal hooks, and thimbles. One pot of pickled kidney beans had shattered, and he picks through the shards, slipping little bites of the vinegary mush and enjoying the salt. He wipes the shelves dry and sorts the jars by how full they are, left to right, the heaviest ones on the top shelf.

190

Scrabbling on that top shelf for a dropped lid, Davy feels a soft package. He thinks about leaving it. After all, white men have their magic too, and Davy has been fairly warned about meddling in the unknown. His mother says the devil comes in shapes we don't already know.

But now he is a worker and he has been told to fetch something, and he might get paid for it. On the farm, they are pounding the rice that was harvested in September. They'll be pounding the rice until the new year and the fields are ready for clearing again, and Davy isn't yet old enough to contribute his labor. They have calculated the age at which a boy slips over the threshold between diminishing risk of mortality and increasing strength. He'll keep his wages until his master finds out, and then he'll hand some of them over. Between his eggs for sale and his straightening a man's hearth room, he figures he can soon buy his mother, and then she'll buy him, and then they'll buy a proper house. Right by the water, where he's never allowed to play.

He holds the parcel in two hands, away from his body, and walks it out of the hearth room, past Mrs. Randolph — who sits back on her heels and watches the procession — and all the way to town, the parcel leading the way. It flops heavily, like a dead cat. It makes Davy's spine twitch.

One evening a man comes to visit John in his empty house, a sailor from his sailing days. The man had asked in town for him and found his way here. He knows nothing of a wife and child, but says that John looks well, for he still has both his legs and seems well fed.

"I haven't been to sea in years," John says. He doesn't count the four days with his daughter.

"That's it, then," he says, "the look of a landed man."

John finds some bread and a jug of old beer, and his friend counters with rum from his sack. They toast their old friend Tom, who is confirmed dead, hanged for hoarding limes.

"It could have been me," the sailor says, and John nods. The pirate's motto. The lines walked between life and death were mere filaments.

The man slides into false tales of bounty — gold and virgins — and paints the air in the dark room with his hands. The monsters were larger, the plagues were viler, and the Spanish had more cannon than he'd ever seen. But when the night finally falls and the rum he brought is mostly drunk, his stories fade, and John fails to fill the silences. The men soften, grow tired, are melancholy together in a pleasant way.

"I'll tell you, I've given it all up, same as you," the man says. "I'd get letters from my old father, worried about me, thinking I'd fall overboard at a gust of wind. So I put up my ropes and bought a little land in the territories. It's nice there, plenty of space and work to go around."

John leans forward and rubs his knees. "What sort of work?"

"Trees, mostly. You can cut them down for days and not see any less." The man puts his fists together and

192

gently swings his hands back. "Chop, chop. All day, for days."

"Just men out there?"

"Oh, and a few wives. It's dangerous if you don't keep an eye open, but they teach you how, and there aren't many mishaps. The men who get hurt are those busy thinking about other things, about families at home and the price of tobacco, but I've nothing else to think on, so it suits me well." He stretches his feet out in front of the fireplace, which is unlit, hoping this might prompt his host.

John is not cold. Or rather, he has come to accept the chill as his due. He could leave. If there is nothing left — and surely there is nothing visible left — he could save himself. There is a suction of pain here that will not release him, whether he is in his house or behind the store's counter or knee-deep in reeds, looking out at the dawn for traces of lost things. The desire to preserve himself is a recent impulse and, he thinks, a healthy one. It is a different kind of giving up.

"There are still jobs?" John asks.

"Some of the men are always moving on. I'm leaving myself, back to Maryland now that my father's finally passed on. You're interested? I could give you the names of a few men who'd serve you well. You'd like it, being just a lone man yourself."

John pours the last drips of rum into their cups. The walls seem plastered with Tabitha's handprints; every surface still rings with her presence. He has trouble believing that his visitor is immune to the girlishness of this house, and yet he cannot correct him. He is alone.

"How far out?"

"A day past the western edge of Carolina. There are paths well laid by now, some Indian. I wouldn't make the trip by myself, of course. Any number of things could get you. But find a man to take along, and you'll both do well for yourselves." He looks around, sniffs. "This is a fine house here, but you could claim a hundred acres soon as sneeze. Men are moving west, and that's going to be the way of it, I figure. I'm not a sentimental man, but it's lovely country too. Beautiful in the mornings. Cool."

John gives the visitor the parlor sofa, for there is no longer a mattress in his own room, and he pulls a blanket for himself to where Tab once slept, spreads it on the floor by her window. The glass is still smudged. From her fingers? Her small nose? He holds his palm an inch away from the pane and closes his eyes. Each day that she isn't raised from the dead, the weight of her memory grows heavier around his neck. What is there left of her to abandon?

In the night he dozes and wakes, and wonders what leaving means.

The slaves have moved from the fields to the barn, where the rice is dried, threshed, and winnowed. Soon they will begin the pounding, which will last most of the winter. Moll has trouble keeping up the pace, and when she becomes dizzy, two men carry her outside and rest her against a corner of the barn. Moses, who cannot stop, sends word for Davy; the boy comes with water and bread to revive his mother.

194

He dips a rag in the water and places it on top of her head. She reaches a weak hand up and moves it to her forehead and cheeks, the back of her neck. The October days are still warm, and the barn heats up with all those bodies.

"Someone said you might be —" He pats his belly and puffs out his cheeks.

She looks over at her son with suspicion.

"So? Are you eating enough?"

"I'm eating enough," she says. "Lord help us both if there's another one in me." If Moses touches her again, she'll cut his manhood off. She is done with him, with people taking what is hers.

"Well," Davy says, reaching over for her hand, "I don't mind babies. Maybe you'd even have a boy."

"Heaven forbid." She stands, leans one hand against the wall. "Come here."

Davy ducks away, thinking it's a game.

"Come here," she says.

He looks disappointed. He takes the rag from her shoulder, wrings it out, dips it in the water again. "Don't get silly," he says.

She wraps one hand around his neck, pulls him close. She is still just taller than her son.

He wriggles within her grasp.

Moll does not think of herself as a demonstrative mother. She does not heap praise upon her children; her attentions are aimed at keeping them out of trouble. Her son and the daughters that trail after him like stepping stones are still young, not yet caught in the violence that will become mundane. But what she would tell her son, if she could find the words and if he would sit still enough to hear them, is that he is the reason she still exists. The daughters came because that's what babies do, they come, but none of them answered her doubts the way Davy did. He's the light that keeps drawing her on.

She is glad Helen never met him; the boy is her only own thing, inviolable.

"Get on home," she says, pushing him away. When he laughs, she pinches his nose. "I'm fine, I've just been working too hard."

"Maybe you're getting sick."

"And maybe I'm getting sick, that's right."

He tucks the jug of water under his arm and starts back for the cabins, where he has been cleaning.

"Davy," she says. He turns around. "You're the only baby I want."

John is coming to dinner, and Asa is in the back garden, picking the last of the roses before they are consumed by frost. He prefers the blossoms with petals tightly packed, like women's skirts. Along the kindling fence grows a prairie rose whose single blooms look naked, their golden stamens rude. It was his wife's favorite. His wife, whom he rarely thinks about in these days of new loss. She brought a cutting of the wild rose from her parents' garden and planted the start in the sandy soil behind the house. When it began to flourish, she made Asa build a fence for it, adding pickets as it clambered west and east, reaching for any horizon. She weeded beneath it weekly, coming in only when her fingers were dimpled red with pricks. The thorns were small and crowded on the stem, and their points recurved like cat's claws. She never cut the flowers to bring inside the house, so he does not cut them now. Their color is the same as a woman's lips, flushed, after being kissed. He was not as sweet to her as he could have been.

In the absence of the beloved, there is new space for guilt and should-have-dones. Regret only exists once the opportunity for change is gone. Asa counts a hundred things that might have saved him in God's eyes — small gestures, touches of love. In imagining them, he can almost pretend they once took place. She is sitting in the garden on a little stool, just a few inches above the overgrown grass, her hands resting on her neck. He kneels down behind her and begins to knead her shoulders. He places his cheek against her back. His hands curl around her, and they warm each other in the already warm sun. This is something he never did. Who is the woman in the garden? It doesn't matter; he never held her close.

He weaves some asters into the plucked roses and carries the handful inside. Mrs. Randolph is busy with a sick child, so he has asked Moll to help him with dinner. He brings her the flowers and asks for a vase to put them in. She looks tired, but she takes them and squeezes his hand. Hers is a presence he is still negotiating. It hurts to have a young woman in the house who is as tall as his daughter, who knew his daughter, though she is now ten years absent. When he sees Moll, he remembers Helen as a ten-year-old, chicken-poxed, and then his throat collapses because he remembers that girl is dead. No, it's not her; it's Tabitha. Tab is the little girl. He fights to call up her face. So where is Helen? Ah, Helen is gone too. When Moll brings him the roses in a blue glass vase, he resents the life that still warms her hands, still moves her feet noisily across the stone floor.

With the flowers in the center of the small dining table, and the two cloth napkins spread out beside the wine glasses, and the porcelain bowls waiting for their soup, the room almost looks alive again. Asa sits and rubs the stem of his glass, an act in which he has traditionally found comfort. Within the slim crystal column are two intertwining ribbons, opaque, like drops of ink released into water. His eyes trace them, separating them, tracking their spirals from the glass's bowl to its foot. At the base, the ribbons vanish into a lumpy pool, clear, with a single trapped bubble. He begins again at the top.

John finds him sitting, hunched over the table, his eyes fixed on his wine glass.

They shake hands and for the first two courses speak of farming and the expected frost and what the General Assembly will decide on rates of export. When Asa's soupspoon trembles at his chin and sends a few drops smattering on his shirt, John looks down. They fall into a silence when Moll brings them saucers of spiced apples. There are men who can sit in peace without speech, but not when a hole the size of a child sits in the room with them. Neither knows how to proceed.

198

They move their apples from one side of the dish to the other.

John starts to speak, but his throat has gone dry and his words turn into a startling cough. Asa flinches, and his spoon flips a slice of buttered apple onto the white tablecloth.

"There's something — excuse me. Something I've been thinking on," John says.

Asa doesn't want to be shouted at when Moll finds the stain on the tablecloth. He eats the fallen slice and pulls his glass closer so the foot covers the brown mark. She won't remember which side he was sitting on.

"I'm finding it difficult," John says.

"The Lord tries us." Asa is not sure what is being discussed.

"I don't believe I can continue an ordinary sort of life. Here."

Asa is adrift again. An ordinary sort of life. He cannot imagine what this means. It is afternoon now, and the sun is cutting through the crystal and sending little shoots of light into the corners of the room. Not all men marry, or have children, and they too make up God's flock. There are roles for all of them in this pageant, surely, and patience is rewarded. Asa must believe God is watching. Reminded of this, he smiles at John with encouragement.

"A man I used to sail with has found a farm inland and a job felling timber. Land is cheap and labor needed. It's easy to start fresh, he says, and build yourself again."

Asa nods. He can see his body from the outside, a picture of tolerance, a modern Job.

"West of the mountains. I didn't want to leave without consulting you. If you needed anything, of course."

"You're going on a trip?"

John runs his hands up and down the wooden arms of his chair. "I'm thinking of buying new land out west," he says. "In the Southwest Territory, near the Watauga. I've got some money saved, and will be paid well to cut lumber from the forests there. Plenty of old hardwoods, more than are left near Beaufort."

"For shipbuilding? No, that's too far for ships, couldn't get the lumber to port."

"It's for building houses, I imagine, and laying roads and fences," John says. "The West is getting bigger."

"Yes, houses. It makes a man, to build his own house." Asa gestures with one arm around the room. "This, of course, was once nothing, just posts and boards."

"I plan to leave next week, if I can get a buyer for my share of the store."

"Why are you leaving the store?"

"I'm going to move to the Southwest Territory."

"The Southwest Territory," Asa says. He frowns. "What about Tabitha?"

John waits to see if Asa has forgotten, if his distraction is in fact senility, but he can't read the older man's face. His guilt flushes him, curdles in his throat. "I don't imagine her ghost will ever leave me."

"You are an optimist?"

Moll comes in to clear the dessert and finds the men looking at each other, mystified. When she asks if she should bring out the decanter, Asa looks up at her, his eyebrows raised into a plea.

"John says he's going to leave us."

"Is that right?" Moll stands with one hand on her hip beside Asa, forming an alliance. "Can't take the sorrow?"

John stands and refolds his napkin with a few quick snaps. "I've been offered a chance beyond this town, and I would prefer to be useful. Excuse me." He walks out to the front porch and sits on a rocking chair, not rude enough to leave his host entirely.

After the span of time a mother usually gives an unhappy child, Moll comes out and sits beside him. "I didn't spend as much time with her as I'd have liked," she says. "She reminded me of Helen, and of course I had my own children to raise. You did a fine job on your own, I wasn't worried about that. But now I do wish I had known her more." She unties the apron from around her waist and rolls it into a ball. "You sure you want to leave him behind?"

"I'm not much use to Asa."

"I imagine it's hard for men to see that they're much use to anyone. He'll be lonelier if you're gone, I'm certain. And you — what'll you do without a friend in the world?"

He is silent.

"And you'll make it out there by yourself?"

"I haven't planned the details of my journey, Moll, but I am not a newborn child."

"Just thought it'd be nice to have a soul to talk to, all that way. If you're set on it, there's little I can say. I do call you a coward, though." She waits, and then briefly touches his arm.

The sea today is flat and looks like a silvered sky. This is what he will leave; this is what reminds him of her.

The back room of the store smells like sweat and cinnamon. Someone has asked for fishing line and Davy stands in the doorway, scanning the crowded shelves above the limp mattress for rolls of horsehair and gut string. The room is dark, and unidentifiable objects pick up glints from somewhere. He is afraid to go in.

"No, sir," he says. "All out of that."

The customer looks at him suspiciously.

"We have plenty of currants, though." Davy extends his arm behind him, showing off the wall of small jars. "Do you have a wife? My own mother would kiss me for some currants. All the ladies are using them in cakes. Then of course we get to eat them, don't we? You can't go wrong with currants, sir."

The man walks out of the store without speaking, and Davy pulls down his cheeks to make a face at the man's back.

John returns to find the boy digging into the side of the counter with a pocket knife. "Carving your name?"

"Folk won't buy from me."

"I hear it's the other way around. Didn't I show you where goods are kept?"

"It looks like some kind of conjure den in there. I've seen eyes looking at me where there weren't no cause to be eyes." Davy squats down behind the counter, illustrating his fear.

"How old are you?" John knows how old he is. He remembers Moll's round shape when he and Helen left Beaufort, and the colicky baby that was just learning to stand and falter when they returned to bear their own daughter into the world. Even at a distance, the boy had always been a marker of Tab's growth, the line drawn just above her.

"Come here," John says. He lights a lamp and hands it to the boy, leading him into the back room. "Stand there while I look for demons." He makes a show of pulling out jars and boxes and digging behind barrels and standing on his toes to peer onto top shelves. "Not a thing."

Davy points down to the mattress, which looks to him like a giant strangled snake. John paws through the sheets and his discarded clothes from yesterday. "That," Davy says, pointing more emphatically at the glistening skin that seems still to breathe.

John picks up the long banner of blue silk, with its veins of pink and green. Since Davy brought it to him, wrapped in brown paper, John has slept with Tab's birthday present every night. In the dark hours, the endless waking night hours, the coolness of the silk on his cheek has reminded him of his daughter's skin before the fever. After the fever. Is her body still cool in its barrel of rum, nestled like an egg deep in its nest of soil? He doesn't think of her often like this, her physical body, its inevitable decay. His daughter is not really there, in that silence. Where, then? In this scrap of wrinkled fabric, twined around his sleeping body? Is she — or a shard of her, a soul — with God? John is tired of looking for her, and cannot stop. Wherever she is, surely Helen is there too.

"It's just a few yards of silk. No ghosts." He holds it out, but the boy dances away.

"That's nothing for a man to get all curled up with. You should give it to a lady who could use it. Bet you could get five dollars for it."

Of course he should sell it. It's empty. He could give it to Davy right now to take to Moll. Give her some beauty in her life. He folds it up and puts it under his arm. "Now tell me where the fishing line is."

In the late afternoon, John hands the boy a rag and sets him to dusting. He sits behind the counter on a stool and watches Davy move his hand along the shelves, in the spaces between boxes, along the tops of jars. John can hear the murmur of a song half-sung. The boy flips the rag with a flourish, as if his life were a pleasure. Moll is right. If John travels by himself, he may not make it past the mountains. He carries instincts within him now that leave little room for hope, for forward movement. It is not impossible that he would find a child-shaped rock to curl around and clutch until the snows came and he was buried under. He needs a guide in the wilderness. A bird to sing him through the dark.

204

He must leave his daughter and yet keep living, to prove it can be done: that man determines his own life, and his sins are his alone.

On Sunday, John finds Asa in church. The older man's head is bowed, and he remains still when the others rise and sing and sit again. John sits behind him and watches the subtle movements of his shoulders, the thin hair gathered in a ribbon at the neck. A few strands tremble when John exhales. The homily floats in and out. Words like *charity* and *tolerance* mean little. A silver hair curls loose on Asa's coat, and John reaches out to pluck it free. He absently winds the hair around his finger and then brushes it to the floor. The woman next to him pulls in her feet to avoid it.

The door of the church has been left open for the cool November wind, and the air carries with it the hushing sound of water. The curate's voice rises above it like a buoy, and the congregation nods. Asa's head remains bent, his body folded. John thinks of an even older man sitting in the sky watching these obeisances. What can a single man do, even if he is God? Take your loved ones, and then take your pain away? There's no purpose to that game beyond whimsy. John stands. Taking hold of the pew in front of him, he gropes past several women, stepping on a foot, pardoning himself. It's colder in the sunshine. He wraps his coat more tightly and waits for the service to end. A horse tied to a post has eaten all the grass she can reach and begins to snort. John smooths her neck and tugs out the knots in her mane. She chews the edge of his coat thoughtfully. John can still hear the curate, testifying to an unknowable omniscience.

The faithful are always happy to be released; they file out into the morning with plans for airing the rugs, visiting the sick negroes, writing overdue letters to cousins. John catches Asa's eye, and the two men separate from the crowd, walking slowly toward the waterfront.

"You should wait for spring," Asa says. "The passes will be snowed in before long."

"I'll cross before then."

"The dirt will be frozen when you start building a house."

"Better hard ground than mud. Come, there's no reason to stay here through the winter." A pair of fishermen are cleaning their nets by the wharf and nod as John and Asa walk past. Their hands are chafed and red, and one man whistles. There are scenes that will not be repeated on the far side of the mountains. John stops when he sees a dried sand dollar and almost picks it up for Tab.

"I'll sound like an old man, but don't you think of being lonely?" This may be the first time Asa has said the word aloud. Did he ever think of it when he was younger? He remembers missing his mother when she rode to visit friends, but he has not felt like such an aching human fragment since boyhood. Now all he sees are the open-mouthed gaps in his life, the absences that threaten to swallow him. Is he alone in his loneliness too? This man, the husband to his daughter, his grandchild's father, who stares at a sand dollar on the ground with an expression that could be melancholy — he is now uncoupled from Asa, and is probably grateful. Asa bends to pick up the white shell, which weighs as much as a bird. "Take it. You'll miss the sea."

All grown men miss the sea.

"You still own Moll, don't you?" John rolls the sand dollar between his palms as they turn back toward Long Ridge. "Cogdell didn't take her on after the marriage with Moses?"

"No, she's still mine."

"I was wondering if I could make a purchase of you."

"You want Moll?"

"Her son, actually. The oldest."

They have passed the waterfront and are on a tree-lined path that winds northeast to Asa's plantation. Half the leaves are gone, and those that are left shiver in the wind. Asa does not consider himself a sensitive man, but he twists away from this proposal. "It would be a hardship for Moll, surely."

"I have reason to believe the boy would not mind. It's your decision, of course."

"My decision? Well." This seems unfair. Asa fiddles with a button on his coat, worrying a loose thread. Moll hasn't brought her son around in years, but Asa still spots him on warm nights, sneaking through the fields with a little gang of howling children. "I can't see he'd be much use to you. You'd have him carry your bags, that sort of thing?"

"Better to have two men on a trail than one. And he can help me break land for the farm."

"The farm?"

"When I get out there, get some land."

"What will you grow?"

"He'll be useful."

Asa tries to remember where his son-in-law is going. Somewhere west. He can't grow rice if it's dry, but maybe cotton. Pines, they have pines everywhere, but it sounds as though he'll be cutting them down. No use in teaching him turpentine. What would John find to talk about with a little negro boy? But then again, almost all of it is still unsaid. They could talk for days and not reach the end. Before they arrive at the house, he shakes John's hand and promises to consider it.

Returning to town, John tosses the sand dollar into a hedge of fruiting holly.

Inside, in a soft chair, with a cup of tea in his hand, it seems to Asa that John is saying yes, he is lonely, he does miss his child, he does want to carry some history with him. It isn't Asa's place to deny him comfort. And what he failed to say was that Moll belongs to Helen. Belonged. So the boy is rightly John's, in any court where property is apportioned. In a higher court, Asa has his doubts. Who most deserves a child? He rests his hands on the arms of the chair and closes his eyes, waiting for something to fall into his open palms. He wants to fill whatever holes riddle John, for he knows that no one is left to fill his own. The light beyond his eyelids fades. He sleeps.

"How far?"

John is sweeping the store while Davy sits on the counter and swings his legs, kicking the wood with his heels. He and the boy have started a pile of items he'll need for the journey; a man from New Bern is coming this afternoon to pick over the rest of the stock. The owner of the building has agreed to look for another renter, but John must earn his capital back from the bags of flour and packets of coffee beans. He's selling the house in town to a landowner who wants a wedding present for his daughter. He also has a little money saved from Helen's dowry, the belated sum that Asa gave her when she returned from sea, full-bellied and back-sore. Browned and smiling. Who could have denied her? Always hungry for the next experience, Helen would have given him her blessing, would have wanted the money to be employed in just this way. "It's of no use to *me*," he can hear her say, the back of her hand cool on his cheek. "What would I trade it for, where I am?" He strains to see her body; he begs his reverie to include Tab by her side. The women together, not grim and pale, or lost, or dead.

"I said how far?"

John leans on his broom and watches the dust motes rise in the columns of light: even the inanimate is still alive. The only cure for thought is action. "Four hundred miles or so."

"Would we both have horses?"

"I wouldn't make you walk. I'll toss you on the mule beside the bags and canteens." He pushes the door open to sweep the dirt into the street. A woman crosses to the far side of the road.

"I'd want room and board and pay."

"Pay?"

"I won't be forced to do things," Davy hops down from the counter and digs an almond marchpane from a glass jar. He sucks on it while watching John's face.

"Won't your mother miss you?"

"She's got my sisters to fuss over. I only get into trouble anyway."

"Well, I certainly don't want any troublesome boys along."

Davy stands a little straighter and pulls at his shirt. "I was only fooling, sir. I'd work very hard. As long as I'm compensated."

"Where did you get these words?"

"My mother tells them to me in case. I should be prepared to take advantage of fortune."

"Do you know what fortune is?"

"I suppose it's you taking me to the territories, sir. With compensation." Davy takes another candy and begins rubbing down the counter with an oiled rag. He has no allegiance to the sea, has never learned to swim, does not look south to the water when he walks along Front Street. He has always looked straight ahead, and is only interested in things he's never seen.

Something blows through the front door with a bang, and Asa spills his soup. The tablecloth is collecting stains, patches of muted color. His hands have taken on a tremble since the burial. Even his comb wrenches out accidental strands at his morning toilet. He always seems to be wavering. His coat is hard to button. The pen jumps around in his fingers. He rubs at the small golden spot on the cloth, licks his finger, and rubs again.

Moll walks in, and before her angry skirts swirl to a halt, she points her finger and says, "You son of a *bitch.*"

There is a precision in this gesture he cannot avoid. He sinks an inch into his seat and wipes his mouth with his napkin, looking up at her like a schoolchild.

"You who *know* better."

Mrs. Randolph appears behind her, lurching and apologetic. "Please," she says, holding one arm out toward the door, as if Moll could be herded.

Asa raises a hand and nods at the older woman, who steps back, thinking of her bread almost done on the hearth. He stands slowly and reaches to pull a chair out from the table.

Moll's eyes are red, her face swollen. "What price are you taking? Is this some vengeance?"

"Do sit down."

"I'd rather be whipped. What would your daughter say?"

Asa sits again and twists one of his rings. The fire behind him is keeping his back warm, a very human comfort. He has been a diligent master, and keeps his slaves in firewood, cloth, and fresh meat on Sundays. He is not a barbarian. He didn't sell Moll to her husband's master because he wouldn't fully trust Cogdell's self-discipline, his Christianity. His few slaves lead better lives here, surely, than on plantations of rice or tobacco, and certainly they are better taken care of than if they had been left in native Africa, victim to lions and who knows what other creatures. And hadn't

Helen taught them their letters and some morality? Looking back on this now, he can see its value. They were raised as Americans.

"I thought you might see it as an opportunity," he says. This is a word that has led men by the nose to battlefields, women to the altar.

Her hands grasp in the air. "I wish you had something you still loved that I could take from you."

"I don't see it like that at all. You have other children, haven't you, and John says the boy's keen to go."

"You heartless son of a *bitch*."

He stands and pushes past her into the hallway. "I will not have a conversation like this."

"You *had* a child," she says.

He is on the porch, and she has followed him. "I'm sorry," he says, avoiding her eyes. "The boy seems eager, and John I think could use the company."

She begins to nod. "I see. I see. A substitute child."

"Nothing like that. It's hard on the road, and he'll be starting a new home."

"Hard for a man to ride a hundred miles by himself."

"It's been hard for all of us, without her."

"Take what's mine, then. All those years Helen preached to us, said we were all people, same as each other, that was a lie." Her last words come out through tears.

"I should remind you that your son is mine to sell. This isn't really a matter for discussion."

She drops to her knees, and he steps back, afraid. She places her palms on the porch and begins dragging them across the floorboards. The old wood, which has needed new paint for years, splinters into her hands.

"Stop that."

She drags and drags her hands. Her face twists with pain.

He reaches down to grab her shoulders. He knocks her arms away. He is on his knees, pinning her wrists together. She is keening, making childbirth cries. He is terrified, but her wrists are now limp in his hand as she sobs. "I'm sorry," he says. "I'm sorry." It is cold, and he can see the beads of blood congeal on her shaking palms.

When she has gathered her breath again, she looks into his eyes, inches away. She holds up her hands to show him. "I will not live like this," she says. "You cannot make me live like this."

The store is almost empty now. The man from New Bern has carted away most of the large boxes, and other goods have been sent to Charleston by sea. In the back room, John and Davy fill knapsacks with provisions. Davy puts a jar of candies into his bag, and when he goes to fetch something from the main shelves, John pulls it out again. The boy has brought all his clothes from home — two pairs of trousers, two linen shirts, an overcoat, and a man's hat, probably stolen from his father — and has rolled them into a ball. John untangles them, folds them into neat squares, and stacks them in his bag.

"Can I stay here tonight?"

John sits back on his heels and studies the room. He will have to be careful about overloading the mules. Whatever he has told Asa, he is not looking forward to crossing the state at the beginning of winter with an eleven-year-old boy. But it is the only way to survive. The thought of that sharp discomfort is preferable to the weight that swamps his hollow chest every time he rounds a street corner or faces the open sea and doesn't find his daughter. Will Moll miss her son this much? No, no one can miss a child as much.

"You'll spend tonight with your mother, and I'll see you here at dawn."

"What if she kills me before then?"

"Then I'll have more room to carry biscuits." He hands the boy some parcels of dried meat wrapped in paper and twine. "Split these up between our sacks. I'll take a last glance at things."

The main room looks smaller empty. He finds a box of nails in the far corner of a shelf, and a roll of tallow candles. Underneath a hat stand lies a pile of mouse droppings that the broom didn't catch. Tab used to hang from the arms of the stand when she was little, monkey-size. Behind the counter he finds the first scratchings of a boy's name: *D-A-V*.

In the back room again, Davy has his hands wrapped in the yardage of blue silk.

"What are you doing digging through my bag?"

"I thought you said you were giving it away." Davy stuffs it back into the satchel and replaces John's clothes and drinking cup and the apples and packs of meat. His voice gets quieter. "Can't figure what you'd do with it. Waste of space. Could take an extra blanket."

"What's that?"

"Sure would be easier to spend the night here, sir."

"Out you go. I'll finish up. Get, get." John shoos him from the room. Davy yells a protest and then pounds his hand in a bouncing rhythm along the counter on his way out. The force of his exit leaves the room humming. Children, even the most shy and tongue-tied, spill all their vibrancy out into the world. There are no reserves, no deep wells where emotion sinks and is buried. It takes all of John's energy just to reach the open door and pull it shut.

In the morning, he will force himself to move. He will keep moving until his legs give out, and then the ghosts will carry him home.

Moses shaves the sides of a wooden last into the fire. He has gotten too many burns from smithing and so is practicing to be a cordwainer's assistant, but he cannot shape a proper mold. When he tries to fit it into his own shoe, the leather sides collapse. The shavings are wet with oil and send sparks caroming through the fire. Moll sits on a mattress and braids a rug out of fabric scraps. Neither looks at Davy. The boy has taken off his stockings and is picking at a boil on his toe.

"You can't tie me up," he says.

Moll reaches down to pull another twist of fabric from the bag. She leans her head back to stretch the soreness from her neck.

"I'm not a baby either." Davy tosses a sock across the room. On the second mattress, two young girls roll onto each other and kick.

Moll stops her hands and looks at him. Moses shifts on his stool and releases a grunt of frustration. His knife is too dull. When he puts away his last and crawls onto the large mattress, Moll blows out the candle for him and moves to finish her strand by the hearth. Davy scratches at his legs. There are too few things in the cabin to occupy his hands. He scoots over to the cradle where the baby sleeps and rubs his fingers in her hair. Moll slaps the floor twice and Davy pulls his hand back.

"You're never going to let me grow up," he says.

"Shh."

He comes closer to the fire and begins separating the strips of cloth. He bends into her ear. "You heard what Daddy said."

"He's not the boss of you."

"The man's giving me wages. I can buy my freedom in a year."

She shakes her head.

"You don't want me to be free. That's it."

Moll bites on a piece of fabric and tears it with her teeth. She wipes her nose with the back of her hand, and then her eyes, and then she puts down the rug and leans her head onto her knees. Davy reaches out, but doesn't touch her.

"Mama," he says.

She can't say what she wants. What can a mother like this want for her child? It does no good to tell him he's breaking her heart. He will blow away from this town, out of her arms, will always be a boy, fighting out of wherever he is. She lifts her face and wraps her arms around him and rocks him until his shoulder is wet with her tears. God has never seen her family. The catechism that she learned and repeated until Helen stopped correcting her was always a lie. Does she believe in the resurrection of the body and life everlasting? Hasn't she died a hundred times and seen no resurrection? On the other side of this life, on the other side of slavery, on the far side of this sea, what is there waiting? Emptiness; it's all she's ever seen. In the morning, her son will ride into that blank and will not return. Is it freedom if she's not there to witness it? Is it love if it has no object present?

After she wraps him in a blanket next to his sisters, she sits with her hand on his back, making figure eights, until he falls asleep. She knew a woman who cut the ropes inside her son's ankles so he couldn't walk. Couldn't work, couldn't be sold, couldn't stand for a whipping. She fed him her own portions for a year and taught him how to write and slept with her hand in his until one morning he crawled into the river with weights around his waist. That was not a life. Moll touches the boy's feet, feels the thin muscles webbed down to his toes, the thick cord at his ankle. She tucks the blanket over them and rubs them until she thinks they're warm.

John is not a bad man. He is stealing her child — he is purchasing her child, which is worse. He loved Helen, and he loved the little girl. But it is not always in white men to love beyond that. She has no choices here. She prays, forgetting that she has dismissed God as a fraud. "Thy kingdom come," she whispers. She begs. "Thy kingdom come."

Halfway through the night, she wakes with the baby's cry. She has fallen asleep in an awkward drape over Davy's legs. When she sits up, her back shoots with pain. She crawls to the cradle to give the child a breast. All her children are killing her. She doesn't know how not to love, and she will die from it. And God will take her wherever he pleases, and she releases herself to this. If it is more pain, she will recognize it. If it is emptiness, it will be welcome. Just let him bring his kingdom soon.

Asa wraps his blanket around his shoulders and leaves his house, making his way slowly down the front stairs in the darkness. He can almost see his father standing in the uncut grass, squinting at the structure that has risen where his boards and posts once were. Who will be left to climb these steps, to have these visions? Now in the grass himself, Asa stops. He has forgotten his shoes. Like a child. He brushes his feet through the lawn, not minding the damp, and follows the path that winds west through the forest on the way to town. The dirt is studded with pebbles and pine needles and sharp bits of leaf that scrape against his feet. Closer to the water, the trees thin out; the oaks here are half-size and writhe away from the wind off the water. The arms reach desperately inland. He remembers another walk, a dozen years ago or more, with Tab. No, it would have been Helen. She had climbed a tree, called it cheerful. Near the top, she raised her hands and moved them in a slow dance. Her limbs and the tree's like seaweed. Asa had smiled, and sometimes as he walked to town in later years it did seem like a whimsical sort of gnarl. At night, though, there is no mistaking.

He stops before he comes to the first houses and rests on a rock that someone has rolled close to the water. Across the moon-tinged channel, the shoals seem like a mirage of dry land. A wild horse left by the Spanish grazes on sea oats. Her snorts carry over the surface of the water to Asa. In the night quiet, he can almost hear her teeth at the roots of the grass.

If he had asked John to move to Long Ridge, perhaps he could have kept him here. The man might have wanted just a gesture of company. Instead, he's taking himself and a young boy into an endless unknown. Traveling west is no better than traveling east, for all the monsters one could meet. This is some men's way of living, though Asa will never comprehend it. There is only satisfaction in stability; one only grows when one is steadfast. He could try again with John. Keep him at the house a month and teach him how to tap pines, and maybe he would begin to settle. Asa could show him how. He could raise him.

This is the hole in him talking. Though he is grieving now, patience, faith, and the will to repeat his daily motions are bound to bring him peace again. He cannot save other lives, is not responsible. Family is illusory. There is God, and there is man. There is the earth, and there is the sea. There is that moon, this horse, the wet grass in his toes. If there are worms in the soil, it is not his place to see them.

They stop at Long Ridge in the morning. Davy waits with the horses and mules while John walks up the front staircase, which in his courting days once seemed insurmountable; now it's just another barrier to be climbed. Asa comes to the door in a dressing gown. John refuses to step inside but holds out a small box.

"I don't mean to leave you. That's not my intention."

Asa takes the box.

"I'll write, if you'll let me."

"Will you stay?"

John looks at him without expression.

"Then. I don't begrudge you a new life. We take our own paths." Asa wraps the gown tighter with one hand against the dawn air. He is tired, and his feet are sore. "We all want to end up someplace different."

"Heaven, isn't it?" John smiles. Asa looks older in his sleeping cap. The light dips into the wrinkles at his eyes, the furrows cut around his mouth. He will probably not see Asa before he dies. The thought reminds him of everyone else he cannot see again, and floods him.

Asa picks at the string around the box, but John stays his hand.

"Open it later. I wanted to say farewell."

Asa looks past him to the lawn below, where Davy is trying to catch his own horse's flicking tail. "Nice to have a young one."

220

"I want to thank you for giving me what you did. For your daughter."

"I said I don't begrudge you."

"What we felt — what we are feeling now — it's not so dissimilar. It will be easier when we're not here to remind each other."

"And this you're certain of."

"When we find each other after all this, you'll tell me everything was all right."

Asa takes a step back into the hall. It is too early for this; it hurts. Easier to keep closing the door, to stay still, to pray.

John holds out his hand to shake.

Asa stands in the door until they wheel their animals and start for the north. Their road flashes before him — the forests and open prairies and the endless jumbled mountains — and when the boy lets out a whoop, two egrets burst from the marsh and glide toward a horizon he can no longer see.

Inside the box is Helen's small face, painted in simple colors on a piece of ivory. It is the face she wore on that summer day when her muddy shoes sat by the door, and her bare feet running from the parlor to the porch sounded like the steps of a child. Innocent, he had not known she was in love; the thought of waiting for this proof of her affection had charmed him. Had he forgotten about it? No, because it does not surprise him to find the miniature in his hand, all these years later.

He closes the front door and kneels on the rug in the hallway and places his hands together. He could pray for the children he has lost, or John, or the woman whose son he has sold, but his heart is quiet now, and all he can manage is a few murmurs for his own soul, may it be held and kept.

CHAPTER
SEVEN

The dirt runs through Cogdell's fingers. It's pale brown, sand mixed with loam. He picks out the pine needles and peels off the papery red cap that holds the fascicle together.

"Hasn't been well tended," he says, looking up at Asa, who leans against a trunk.

"Suits fine for trees."

"Not much turpentine business after the war, I'll bet." Cogdell stands and toes over the bare patch. "Not much help, either. How many do you own?"

"Four, but I hire enough so everything gets done. It's brought in plenty."

"Getting too old, is that it?"

"There are other things to be done."

"With everyone leaving town, there's not much. In ten years, I'd be surprised if the whole place wasn't turned into a big plantation. Ship everything upriver or by sea. No need for anyone to live here at all. We'd be better off in Wilmington where the ladies are." He waits for Asa to respond, but the older man is still looking at the ground. "Since your son-in-law left, you can't even buy a good pound of coffee."

"They're stocking it again."

"Seems like everything's flowing out of Beaufort on the tide. You're wise to sell." Cogdell turns back to the house, slapping his palm on the trunks as he passes them. Asa thinks he'll have a hard time washing the resin off. "I'll need to dig channels through here to bring enough water for rice. The dirt's been dried out from all these roots. Prices have gone up since the war, but we're still selling it cheaper than the Indies, and it cooks better. That's what I hear. There are men by New Bern who are even shipping overseas." He doesn't look behind him to see that Asa has stopped at the edge of the pines, reluctant to step out into the open.

It is early March, and the soil has recently thawed. The hardwoods are bare or budding. Asa has pulled his hat low and turned up the collar of his coat, but his ears are still exposed, and they ache in the wind. Even with the disturbances of men, who each year clear the undergrowth beneath the pines, the acres are once more spilling the first wildflowers. They appear like new coins. Trillium, jack-in-the-pulpit, mayapple. By the house, yellow jessamine hangs in the top of a small oak and smells like satin. These are the things his wife would have noticed, so Asa notices them in her stead.

Inside the house, Asa draws up the agreement for the back section of land; he is selling half instead of a third, but he'll still have enough trees left to make a few dozen barrels a year. Cogdell reads over the paper, following the script with his finger.

"Fifteen acres," he says. "Doesn't seem like much."

Asa points his quill at the paper. "You'll get the land and the five thousand trees too, to do with as you like.

224

Always a market for lumber. You've been wanting to stretch the rice fields out as long as I've known you."

Cogdell scratches his cheek, then signs. They shake hands, and Asa walks him down the back stairs again. A dirt footpath has been rubbed from the small garden over the creek to the neighbor's lands. It passes through the slave quarters and the row of empty cabins. Even from here, they can hear strains of song from the fields, where men and women pull through soil and muck to make furrows for the seed. A spotted hen sits at the base of the stairs, ruffling her feathers in a dirt patch, and doesn't move when Cogdell shakes his shoe at her. The men step around her.

"You'll be selling the rest before too long," Cogdell says.

"That may be."

"There's no use in holding on to land out of pride. A man has to learn to be on his own."

The men have never been close as neighbors. There have been few shared suppers. Cogdell's wife never approved of the women's behavior at Long Ridge and told her friends that she sometimes saw ghosts in dresses walking through the pines at night. Asa's wife thought the woman was shrewish. Asa will tell her about this latest impudence. She'll say they don't need any more friends, and will squeeze his knee. This is a great intimacy.

But when he climbs the stairs again, the house is dark and quiet. The only fire is in the kitchen hearth. It's on shaky kindling legs.

Mrs. Randolph takes Asa's hands and plunges them in the bowl of milky water. "Nothing to be scared of," she says, and adds the soaked yeast and the quarter pound of butter. "Go on, break it up with your fingers." She mixes two eggs in another pan, forking the yolk into yellow strings, and pours them into Asa's bowl. He feels the pleasures of childhood, of direct contact with the forbidden. He actually remembers very little of being young; most of his memories he created, to show how far he's come. Did he even love his mother and his father? There were few embraces. His father had been a servant as a boy; he always expected Asa to do better, and Asa's son to own the whole colony. But Asa didn't have a son, and his parents were no longer alive to see what Long Ridge was, or what it was becoming.

Mrs. Randolph dumps the flour in, and his hands become weary as the dough stiffens. She covers the bowl with a cloth, and they sit on stools with cups of tea to wait for the dough to rise. Asa picks at his fingernails, digging the flour out. The fire has been built properly, and the room is warm and smells sweet.

Mrs. Randolph is beginning to feel old and her children are growing up, and she is no longer quite comfortable working at Long Ridge with all the women absent. She stayed on after Helen's death because of the little girl, who needed plenty of mothering when she was young and who continued to visit the big house on Sundays, when Mrs. Randolph would bake her Chelsea buns and show her how to tie ribbons. With only Asa left, it's time to return to her own family. She

226

doesn't believe in hauntings, but she has a sense of being exposed when she's dusting the furniture of Long Ridge. It's a lonely house now. She is sorry to leave Asa in it, but she can train him to take care of himself, and he'll be happier with more to keep him busy.

They talk about Mrs. Randolph's children, and the families who have left Beaufort since the war, and their hopes for a wet spring. When the dough is ready, Asa pulls it into pieces and rolls them between his hands to make little balls, which Mrs. Randolph lines up on a pan. She slides them on the shelf above the fire, and they watch the rolls turn golden. Asa writes down the cooking time on a sheet of paper: quarter of an hour on one side, quarter of an hour on the other. Once he knows how to make bread, porridge and ham for breakfast will be simple. He has promised Mrs. Randolph that he can learn, that he doesn't need to hire a younger woman. She has been gracious in believing him. He holds his pocket watch, glancing from the minute hand to the bread and back. He flips them with a damp rag and Mrs. Randolph nods.

They wrap them in napkins and carry them to the dining room, where Asa cuts and butters them for a morning snack. They have run out of conversation. Mrs. Randolph is glad to be served for once, and she watches Asa's movements as if he were a lady pupil. When he sucks the butter off his fingers before passing her a roll, she laughs. "I think you were meant for a bachelor, sir," she says.

"There is something easier in it."

"I shouldn't have said. But yes, now you needn't mind your steps so much."

"And who's to say I'll take the time to make proper bread? If you visit, you may well find me foraging for scraps in the chicken troughs." Asa smiles at the woman to put her at ease. The rolls are not as good as when she makes them herself, but he doesn't say anything.

"You'll be all right, sir."

He is loath to let her go. She will be the last bird to leave, and his forest will become as silent as winter.

"And what's that one? Right up there, on the crooked branch. Look, I'm pointing."

John shakes his head.

"It's not a woodpecker, I know it." Davy pulls his horse up short and turns its reluctant head around. "Do you see the long tail?"

They are on a trail that circles the settlement and runs behind the logging fields. It is one of the first warm days, and Davy jogs his horse up and back, kicking at the layers of mulch that have broken down after the winter. John is on scouting duty; the man and boy travel the perimeter once a week to look for hostile Indians, whom they never find. Instead Davy pesters him for information about the world — birds, Cherokees, mathematics, ghosts. John is newly aware of his own ignorance.

"We're eating supper with Foster tonight." John is now well ahead on the trail. The boy comes galloping up behind him, passes him, turns sharply with one hand on the reins, the other tossed in the air. John cannot help but smile.

"He only eats turkeys," Davy says, settling down in his saddle again.

"There are plenty of turkeys to be had," John says. "Maybe that's what you saw."

"I think it was a flycatcher. Are they this far west?" John has taught him all the birds he knows, which is not many. In just a few months, with scarce and irregular food, Davy has grown an inch at least, and he feels it. He finds himself extending his limbs, stretching his wrists and ankles and neck at every opportunity, as if by wriggling he could force another inch. Most mornings, he tells John that his bed is shrinking.

The houses here hardly look like houses: rough boards leaned together, notched so they won't fall down in a wind, topped by branches with the leaves still on. They borrowed their home half-built from another man who moved on before the winter, and they've been adding to it piecemeal, which has allowed for Davy's own ideas. He insisted they cut a window in the door so they could see their visitors, coming and going.

"What visitors?" John had asked.

"When we're rich, they'll come," Davy said. "You'll see."

Their shelves hold a few sacks of dry beans and strips of salted venison, and there's a hammer and an auger, and on the top shelf is a wooden box with a metal clasp where Davy puts feathers that he finds. He can't make sense of the other things inside: glass, rope, a little wrinkled rock. John said they were his wife's treasures, so Davy adds his, which are much nicer.

The men in the camp had not allowed Davy to work, but he swore he was sixteen, and John shrugged his shoulders, not saying any different. They spend time in the forests, in their house, in other men's houses, along the trails that dip between the mountains. They stay up late, they take days off, they swim when it is not yet warm enough to swim. They struggle to find food, they work through blisters, their fires spit back at them, and they are almost always cold.

"Who are we eating with for Easter?"

John's horse slows to pick its way down a hill. He takes off his hat and wipes the sweat back into his hair. "I thought we'd make our own meal," he says.

"No turkey," Davy says. "We'd have to make something that didn't taste of ashes. Easter's supposed to be nice."

"I made you a very nice squirrel last week that didn't taste of ashes."

"Excuse me; it tasted like squirrel." Once they are on a flat stretch again, Davy kicks his horse into a trot. "My mother always said we ate well then because of Jesus."

The path opens out into a meadow, and the man and the boy tie their horses to a tree and find a dry spot in the sun to collapse. Davy digs his heels into the grass, kicking out little bits of soil. John crosses his arms over his chest.

"I'll bury you here," Davy says. "When the Indians find us."

230

"What did your mother make?"

"Oh, a ham, and sometimes a cake."

"Where did she get a ham?"

Davy is silent for a few moments. He doesn't know where being a slave begins and ends anymore. He can sometimes forget that there are laws, that there are systems he is subject to. It is too big a world for all that. "I suppose she stole it," he says.

He turns to look at John, but his eyes are closed.

"And what about your mother? Did she make a ham?"

John, half asleep, is surprised. He shuffles through the memories he has kept. He must have had a life before Helen, but was it good? Was it happy? A sediment of grief has compressed any pleasure he might have remembered.

"I think she must have," John says.

"Who'd she steal it from?"

"Or maybe that was only later. She died when I was younger than you, and those that kept me weren't much in the way of money."

Davy turns over on his stomach and begins picking grass. "I miss mine."

John's mother was small, half the size of his father, wore whites and pinks. Was quiet, had some-color eyes. Did she sing? Perhaps she sang at night, under her breath, when he was sleeping. There was a peace in her. And then: years of searching for that again, of climbing toward happiness and falling. Here he lies, in a meadow, beyond even the bounds of his country, recalling the forgotten undertone of his life.

"You better say you miss yours too, or she'll be mad."

"I miss mine too," John says.

"We'll write them letters."

In the cabin once used for church, Moll and the others are silenced by the screams. A few of the slaves still gather here on Sundays to share a quiet company, though there is rarely any formal prayer. An old woman on the back pew turns toward the open door. Two white men are dragging a writhing black body across the fields toward Cogdell's house.

"Who is it?" Moll asks.

The woman doesn't recognize him from this distance; he looks like a dark spider, limbs flailing between his captors. The rest of the congregants gather by the door. A woman cries out. She shoves past the others and runs in the wake of the violence toward the big house. Moll, who has continued these gatherings since Helen's death, guides the others out. She had been reading from Luke: the prodigal son, the shepherd's story, the lost coin. They return to the quarters, where they wait on porches and front steps. Someone makes corn cakes and passes them around. They are all trying not to imagine.

Moses is out hunting, so Moll lies down on the mattress and covers her eyes with one hand. Her daughters are with the granny. Two men ran away last week, and if Moll prayed, she would have prayed for their disappearance. Neither had families of their own yet; there were none abandoned. She was never told of their plans, but she knew, the way one part of the body knows of the hurt in any other part. As the moon faded from quarter-full to a gray shadow of itself, they had all held their breath, avoiding quarrels with the driver so when the time came, the men could slip into the darkness unobserved. And when the two of them left, they waited for them not to come back.

The men would have gone west, into the mountains. They might have found a white man and a black boy still building a house of logs, still plowing the earth for a garden, still cutting lumber for pay. The runaways did what she was too afraid to try. Did she fear for her own body? Had she not acquaintance enough with pain? Did she think she would find her son's corpse, beaten and abused in a ditch ten miles out of town? There are things she doesn't want to know.

It is Abel they bring back to the quarters, his head swollen with brown bandages, his eyes pursed shut. The driver carries him and lays him on his mattress, and the women watch as his mother unwraps the cloth and finds the raw edges where his ears once were. One woman boils water; another tears strips of cloth from her skirt. A few speak in a low, rhythmic language, rubbing their hands and kissing their fingers. Moll stands in the door and watches the women tending Abel's body. His mother stone-faced and methodical. He is no longer conscious and cannot feel the touches on his welted torso and the tender pressure against the holes in his head. His skin is pale brown, with rust running along the shape of his muscles, like a painted man. Fresh blood pools in his collarbone, caught by the light of the candles. Moll turns and walks away.

In the morning, if he wakes, they will huddle around and ask Abel about the other slave, whether he climbed a tree when he first heard the dogs and Abel was too slow. They'll ask how far he got, what the land looked like, where the fresh water was to drink. Some will tell him to try again, and some will hold him close. The loss of his ears will not be his last loss. The white men will take every part of him that does not sow, weed, harvest. He will keep his hands and his feet and his spine. Everything else he will lose.

This is what a mother dreams about at night. She plants herself between these things and her child. She is no defense, but she stands there nonetheless. And that standing is the most protection a man will ever know.

In bed that night, her baby curled between them, Moll asks her husband whether Davy is better off gone.

"Wasn't a choice," Moses says.

"He said he could earn wages, buy his freedom after a year."

Moses turns over, and the baby reaches out her hands to touch his back.

She remembers when Davy was that young. Never cried, was waiting for her every night with smiles, and later, with treasures from his day. A caterpillar, a wooden ball the granny carved him. Once, stolen bread from the kitchens, for which she beat him. Her own mother was sold away, and she never had a father claim her. No one to protect her. She holds the baby's feet.

"In a few months, they would have put him to work here. I couldn't watch him so much once he was in the fields. And you didn't teach him to mind his mouth like he should." She listens to their breathing. "He wouldn't have run away, but he would've been beaten soon enough. And out there, who's to say? I don't know what goes on. It could all come true."

Moses reaches an arm back across the baby to grab Moll's waist. "Sleep," he says. "You got three children left to worry over."

She does, and they happen to be girls. But she cannot bring her mind back to them. "There are wolves in the West," she says, "and he'll be lonely."

The baby's hands slip down from Moses's back; she is asleep. Moll watches their bodies at rest and thinks of her only son, gone. Is his face still whole? No one will ever tell her. Will he remember her when he is a free man, with a free family? She'll be long dead then. When Davy was born, she knew him to be the one sheep among the ninety and nine. The Bible itself told her that the one is the only one that matters.

If there is a place where women meet their children again, if God is the overseer there, she will pray. But only if she can be sure there's such a place. She waits for an answer, for a promise.

The boat is buried beneath a yaupon that in ten years has grown to swallow the peeling hull. Two oars dangle from the side like broken limbs. Asa tries to drag it out, but the keel has sunk into the mud it sits on. He returns with a pair of shears and spends a morning

235

cutting away the lower branches of the yaupon, just the parts that touch the boat, no more. When he is done and his shirt is damp, the boat sits under the pruned shrub as though it were at rest in a bower. Half of the blue paint has been chipped off by wind and age and the curious teeth of mice. The boards are cool. Asa swats at the cobwebs with an oar, twisting them around the paddle and then wiping them on the grass. He makes sure there are no possums under the thwarts and then climbs in and sits. The lowest branches brush his ears. The shade here still tastes of winter.

When he looks up, he sees a small brown bird looking down at him. It bobs its tail while Asa tries to remember its name. It rubs its bill along its wings, like sharpening a knife. In these moments of focus, Asa can forget everything that happened before. Who can he ask to help? He'll have to wait until it rains and then drag it out through the softened mud himself.

It is still light, and Asa is not yet ready for his supper. Strange how schedules melt away when a man lives on his own. He could not even name what day it was; weeks have passed since he signed away the upper acres. No one is there to tell him when things must happen. He'll wait and have some bread and cheese before sleep. Now he returns to his bedroom and collects the linen for washing. He folds the quilt and places it beneath the window. No matter how still he lies, each morning the bed sheets are in knots. He untwists them, pulls them off, piles them by the door. The cotton mattress still has two hollows: his own, deep and knobby, and the shallowest scoop that he alone knows is still his wife. He could turn the mattress over and she would disappear.

He carries the sheets downstairs and outside, along with several shirts, the tablecloth, the basket of dirty napkins. Mrs. Randolph always said he should build a separate laundry, but he had said no, not with just one child. He fills a copper tub with water from the well and bundles the linens in. A stool lies next to the garden wall, overturned by some night animal, and he fetches it and sits next to his task. He puts a hand in; the water is cold and unpleasant. Is there some instrument Mrs. Randolph uses? He gets a wooden spoon from the kitchen and begins to stir. He remembers soap and retrieves the small block from his washstand. He knocks the soap around the sheets with the spoon in the waning light. Think of all the women sitting in gardens from here to New Hampshire, doing what he is doing in the last hour of the day. He is encouraged and stirs with more diligence. When he is tired, he tries to drain the water from the tub, but it is too heavy to lift, so he pulls the wet linens out, which now feel like iron sacks. He throws them over the branches of some low-growing trees and tries to straighten them. The dirt of his body is now being replaced by the dirt of an aging bark, the movement of ants, sparrows' feet.

Inside, the rooms carry an underwater green from the dusk's uncommon light. The sheets outside shiver in the wind. What does that mean? A storm is coming? He should busy himself. He could read the week's newspaper, or write a letter to his old friend from the

Assembly, who has sent him two letters now without reply. But the green fades so slowly, and his body is a difficult thing to move. He abandons the parlor and avoids his desk. He lights one candle for bed, lies down on the bare mattress in the imprint of his own body, and falls asleep before he can remove his shoes. His sleep is the quiet kind, soothed by labor. His only dreams are of bread and cheese.

When the rains come, he is ready. He ties a rope to a hole in the boat's breasthook and wraps the other end around a fence post, unwinding the length of it and walking backward until he is on a line with the yaupon again. When he pulls, the rope tightens around the post; next to him, he can hear the rowboat groaning. The ground is soft and sucks at his feet when he tries to adjust his position. Even with the leverage to support his strength, his body quivers. The rope is hard to hold tightly. John would've had the boat out with a shove.

But the keel digs through the muck, and the rain smooths a path, and the rowboat jolts out of its bower onto a patch of grass, where it looks even more broken and forlorn. Asa wipes his face and climbs into the boat again, this time in the open air. Tomorrow he will sand the oars. Who acquired this boat, to so abandon it? He didn't remember Helen ever using it; she only played in shallow water. It must have been his wife's. Yes, brought from her parents' farm as part of her dowry. His own father, who had helped build three-masted ships, never had a boat of his own; Asa once stole onto a fisherman's dinghy to reach the open ocean and was brought home green and retching. Owning a boat suggested both prosperity and skill, and when his wife said she didn't think they'd need her little rowboat, Asa insisted. It was another acquisition. He should have taken her somewhere in it. Back in the marshes, maybe, at sunset.

He runs his hand along the topside boards where her name used to be painted in white letters. She always had a stomach for the sea, and would sometimes row the short distance to the fish market rather than walk from Long Ridge to Front Street. She was a quiet girl, a holy woman. Asa no longer thinks he was the cause of her death — though it was his seed that had grown and ruptured out of her in violence — how many years ago? Thirty-two, soon thirty-three. That's enough time for fists to become open palms.

The rain slackens; the clouds swell with brightness. His shoes have filled with water. So many things become easier with age. Those dire emotions that wracked his body, pulled it from guilt to rage, from desire to accusation, have been softened, the sharp edges rubbed dull. If Asa has learned one thing in his years of grabbing and planning and blaming, it's that he is nothing but a bystander in God's game. If there is joy in life, it lies in patience, in watching the Lord's creations unfold. He sits in the boat, clean of any anger, and witnesses the rain, the boat, the yaupon, the clouds, the spring. He waits.

She begins to save part of her dry rations in a sack that she tucks between the mattress and the wall, covered by a drape of quilt. The first night, she put the bag under the steps to the cabin, but in the morning it was gone, a few crumbs showing where a raccoon or fox had torn the bag open. These biscuits, these strips of dried fish, this ground corn, she should be offering to her daughters, whose bellies are already hard as drums. Instead, she secrets food within their own home, a cache that a dog could find, if they had a dog. It is already April, planting time. She is in the fields until dark and again by dawn. Their bodies are counted more regularly now. This is not the time when men run away.

But Moll is not a man. She has never known a woman who tried to run, and this gives her a sense of protection; she cannot fail. She has seen enough of the failures to guard against their mistakes: she doesn't share her secret, she doesn't ask for help, she doesn't try to take her children. The women would have asked her how she could desert three daughters to chase one son, knowing that not even Moses would love them once she left. What could Moll have said? That she would chase her firstborn until everyone she ever loved was dead and buried?

The new moon is just a week out. She will carry her sack, the extra food, a cloth for sleeping, her shoes. All her saved-up money she sewed into Davy's coat before he left. She's only made a few coins since from selling eggs, but she doesn't count this as a great obstacle. The road she'll take is a sacred one, the path smoothed for mothers. She has no fear.

After the bell is rung at the end of the day to scatter the slaves, she cooks a poor stew for her family out of the scraps that will not keep. As the girls eat and Moses rubs the calluses on his hands, Moll excuses herself to borrow parsley from a neighbor. She slips down the row of cabins until she comes to Abel's. His mother is already asleep, so they whisper. She pulls an egg from her pocket. She is bartering away her own children's nourishment.

"They knew the path," he says. "Five days out, and they came on horses. We never came out of the forest, and still there were people said they'd seen us, pointed to the hollows where the dogs could get our scent. Every other slave must've come the same way."

"The man you were with?"

Abel chews his last bite of bread, taking his time. "Tried to run. Shot him." He picks up the egg and rolls it from one hand to the other. "When they see you, it's over. You got to stand still and let them take you. They can see about as much as the Lord can."

Moll shakes her head. "Whatever happens is what he plans."

"You believe that?"

She looks at him holding the egg, his clean hands, the twists of flesh where his ears once were.

"This is what he wants?"

She won't know until she finds Davy again. That's the only measure by which she can judge. "You went north through the back of the rice fields and then turned west after the marshes. What other way is there?"

"If I did it again?"

"I just never get to see the country, so I wonder what it's like."

"Straight west, then. I'd get a boat somehow and row straight down the sound, between the shore and the islands. Land a few miles west, or as far as I could get, and then walk down to Wilmington before turning west again. It's mostly swamp, so no one goes that way. All that water, the dogs couldn't smell me."

"Would you really do it again?"

"It'd be harder without the boat; you'd have to go far enough north to loop over the inlets before you could head down the Wilmington road, and there'd still be rivers to cross. Depending on when they noticed, they could get you while you were still in the pines." Abel's mother stirs on the mattress and says something jumbled in her sleep. He doesn't turn to look at her. "Better to have a boat. You had a boat, I almost think you could get away." He looks at her to see how her face changes.

"Good luck to you," she says. "I promise I won't say anything."

"I didn't say I was going anywhere."

She thinks maybe he can hear her blood beat; the veins in her eyelids are thumping. "I can't imagine how anyone would have the courage," she says, and rubs the chills on her arms, trying to look small and weak. "I didn't mean to drag such a story out of you. Just wanted to offer what I could." She stops in the door and looks back at him, sitting cross-legged on the floor. "I wouldn't say anything," she says.

He brings his hand up to cover his mouth.

She nods and leaves. How stupid to have asked him. Her journey now rests precariously on a bond of trust, and she has been conditioned against trust, against dependence on others, having been betrayed by everyone she once believed.

In her cabin, the baby is already asleep, her chin stained with soup. Moll curls around her, picking up her infant hand in hers, playing with her tiny fingers. Moses asks did she not find any parsley, but she pretends not to hear. She has never rowed a boat, but surely she could; she has seen it done and is a fast learner. One oar, then the other, making halves of a circle. This is a fishing town. Somewhere is a boat untied, ready to be taken. God gives what is needed. What is it like to be on a boat in the moving water? How much strength does it take to move forward?

He has run out of meat. The back garden is crowded with loose hens and pullets, but Asa cannot bring himself to slaughter any of them. He has chased a few, but they're clever and he respects their ability to evade him. Once he coaxed a hen on his lap, smoothing down her wings and rubbing the bone between her eyes until she closed them, but it felt like circling his daughter's back when she was sick and couldn't sleep, so he had to let her go. How easily Mrs. Randolph could snap a chicken's neck.

He picks some of the greens and stirs them in a pan with bits of salted ham over the fire. He takes his plate of dinner into the garden. This is what the slaves must eat. The veins of the collards stick between his teeth, and the ham tastes of dust. He could hire a girl from town to cook him something decent once a day, but that would leave him dependent again; he is too old for that. It's time he took responsibility for himself and his dwindling empire. Pull the barricades in. Prepare his soul for the final siege.

His bread, burnt and poorly leavened, soaks up the grease. Asa wipes the bread around the porcelain and considers the plate clean. He returns to the house, puts it back on a shelf for another meal. He should walk up to the acres, or what's left, to check on the new hand, make sure his tools are sharp, but he wanders down to the shore instead. The boat sits where he left it, perched on the last patch of dry land, just above the line of reeds. He takes the oars out — still rough; he forgot to sand them — and prods the boat until it slips down the bank. He steps on a clump of the marsh grass and then into the boat, clutching the oars to his chest. The boat, half on reeds and half in water, rocks beneath him. He is already queasy. With a few more pokes at the bank, Asa manages to shove off. When the rowboat settles into the curve of the sound, Asa holds his breath and waits. A small leak in the bow, out of which a bubble of seawater froths, but otherwise the boat is steady and whole. It floats.

Asa takes a few hesitant strokes. The oars are heavier than he thought, or rather the water is heavier. His muscles strain to provoke any movement in the boat. Tomorrow he'll plug the leak with tar. He crawls up to the middle thwart and puts his shoe over the hole. He can only hold one oar at a time, so he goes in circles, getting used to the feel of his body and the wood in the water, facing first the shore and then the sea and then the shore. He has already drifted several yards past his entry point, so he abandons his lesson and pushes the oar down into the muck to get back to the bank of reeds. He feels like a one-legged crab.

Only when the boat is back on land — half on land, half buried in the wet weeds — and tied to a willow trunk does Asa note the missing oarlocks. He smiles. There is incompetence, and then there is memory loss. Of course a man couldn't wield two oars on his own strength, not even John. Asa pauses at this image. It threatens to carry his thoughts beyond his own limited scope, beyond the small and daily tasks he has set for himself, so he stops. Oarlocks. He will go into town tomorrow and buy some off of the fishermen.

At night, with the one candle he affords himself, amidst the long and wavering shadows that single flame casts, Asa thinks of the boat. The boat — its boards, its little leak, its missing oarlocks — blocks out the faces and the words. The vanishing land, the collards in his teeth, the blame he places on God. The conversations no one would have with him. His open hands, their emptiness. The bodies of the women, the women who begat women who died. His eyes water of their own accord, they wet his pillow in patches, even though he isn't thinking of everything he's lost, though he's only thinking of the boat he's found. Come back to that. Just the boat — its boards, its little leak.

Two days later, Asa makes it all the way from Long Ridge to the wharf. A mile of rowing; Asa's arms tremble, and the boat groans. He buys a bag of paint powder from the store that used to be John's, and some oil for mixing. He will thin it with his own turpentine and restore the boat's old boards. The abandonment beneath the shrubs will be wiped clean. It will be a vessel any man would be proud to own. Should he repaint his wife's name?

On his way back, he wavers between the shore and the sandbars, though the water is calm and responds easily to his oars. But he is a hesitant rower, and his right side is stronger. The boat drifts patiently. On Long Ridge's weedy banks, a woman is standing, her skirts twining between her legs in the breeze. He is lucky he never used to row, for this would surely call forth every memory of paddling home in the evening to find his daughter waiting on the shore. The oars drop in their locks as he tries to recall those scenes, only to find they don't exist. There are ghosts of the dead and ghosts we create from nothing, just to have the company.

It's not Helen but Moll. He wishes she wouldn't watch him struggle toward the bank. She holds out her hand for the rope, and he throws it to her. She pulls him in and wraps the lead around the willow and stands back as he clambers out, one foot sinking into the muck, heaving himself toward the dry ground, falling on one hand. She waits for him to recover. Asa feels red and bullish. His kerchief has come loose and the sun finds the back of his neck, drawing out the sweat. After weeks of loneliness, to be watched like this — he would do anything to be alone again. He pulls at his coat sleeves and wipes his forehead once. He stands at attention and extends one arm toward the house, inclining his head slightly, his feet together. She nods in return and precedes him across the dry lawn to Long Ridge. He looks behind him at the rowboat, askew in the reeds.

She takes one sip of the tea he offers her and returns the cup to the side table. It is the first tea Asa's made, and he is embarrassed. The parlor has a musty smell, and letters and receipts have collected on the sofa. Moll looks at her knees instead.

"I'm surprised you're not needed in the fields," he says.

"It's Sunday."

"Is it?" He wonders why the store was open. After all that, he left the oil and paint in the boat. He looks out the window. Is it going to rain? "I missed church," he says. It's harder for him to remember, now that Tab's gone. He has also been avoiding her grave. She never liked it, sitting on the pew and being faithful. Not like her mother, who had taught them all, father and slave alike. Where had religion been in his own childhood? His mother and father are just hints of people. They worked, he knew that; they labored and built and sweated and slept. First the land, then the small house on posts, then the pine acres. They left him with the seeds to everything he desired. His father had died in a logging accident, and then his mother a few years later of exhaustion, or grief. They were just shadows. His wife had been a glimmer and Helen, finally, had been the light.

He closes his eyes to find her face.

"Why didn't he take me?" Moll asks.

Asa snaps awake. She is looking at him directly. He should have tasted the tea before offering it to her. She'll think he's trying to poison her.

"Your son by marriage owns me and mine, isn't that what you said?"

"John."

"He could've taken both of us."

"A hard journey for a woman," Asa says. "Think of the mountains in winter."

"Who is my master, without him?"

Asa hesitates. He has recently sold the last of his men, using only hired hands for the diminishing acres. Once he sells the rest of the pines, he will have divested himself of human connection. He is severing ties, not seeking them.

"It's you, isn't it?"

"I suppose it makes sense to sell you to Cogdell now that Helen — now that John is gone. Better that you share a master with your husband."

"Will you free me?"

He notices how straight she sits, how clean her hands are, folded neatly in her lap. Her hair pulled away from her face and bound in a red cloth. Her hazel eyes, their streaks of brightness suggesting a slave owner in her ancestry. He was never such a man, though he gave her to a man she didn't love, then stripped her of a son. We make choices in order to make it to the next day. What does he owe her?

She stands up. "Will you free me?"

Why won't he? Even now, he tracks his profits, keeps a tight hand on the money from the land sales, the sales of men, the last few barrels of turpentine. He is conserving, not giving things away. He cannot say who the money is for. John? Even the little slave boy, in due time, if he turns out right. But it is a process; wealth must be earned, not taken. He worked for years, piling, piling, to prove this.

"I have great affection for you, Moll," he says.

She nods, urging him on.

"Freedom — I believe freedom would put you in a difficult position, hard for a woman to sustain. If it's what you sincerely want, however, I think Helen would have encouraged me to provide a way." He is loath to involve himself in anything beyond his own walls. He is hoping she sees his discomfort.

"I agree. I believe my freedom would honor her memory." There is no tool she will not use. She supports herself with a hand clenched on the back of the sofa.

"Yes. Well. You may be right. Here: I can speak to some of the families in town about purchasing your eggs and produce. I will even give you some of my own chickens to start. You will want to be careful about saving your money — don't let Moses get a hand on it — and with other jobs added, I think in a few years you might collect a nice sum."

There is a quiet to the room that seems impenetrable, for all his talking.

"You want me to buy myself."

She is still standing, so Asa gets to his feet defensively. "That seems only fair."

"Did *you* ever purchase the right to see your own children?"

"I have no children," he says.

"And I wonder why God took them from you."

Hasn't he wondered this too? It shouldn't twist him so, to hear someone else name it.

"Get out," he says. He begins to leave the parlor himself, to search for some emptier room. "Get out." He is in the hallway, leaning against the doorjamb to the dining room. He hears her footsteps behind him. The sound of any woman's feet causes him pain now. He is already sorry for having shouted. "Please," he says. He has no sense of what God wants him to do. Waiting so patiently to be guided, surely his own faults cannot be counted against him. It feels like he is being left behind, every day, again.

The front door opens, and she leaves. The house is quiet. The tea in its cup is still. He climbs the stairs to his bedroom. From the window, through the scrub of trees by the water, he can see the prow of his boat, its boards brown and blue. The sea beyond is endless, and empty.

The baby has a cold. Her eyes close and her tiny hands jerk up in pain when she coughs. Moll covers her forehead with a wet cloth and rocks her as she tries to mix a biscuit dough for dinner, but the baby won't settle. Moll passes her to one of the older girls. She is using up their flour ration so that she'll have extra for the road. They will be left with very little. There are women here who will find them and tend them; hers are not the first children to be forsaken. She doesn't worry if Moses will love them, because it doesn't matter.

She saw the boat. All she had seen for days was phantom boats, and then there was Asa in a battered dinghy, struggling to shore. She made her plea, though she must have already known what he would say. There are bridges of sympathy that even good men cannot cross. That was it, that was the last hope, and now her way is clear and righteous. Helen had told them, on those hot Sundays in the cabin, that all their suffering was but steps on the ladder to paradise; it was evidence of faith, of God's favor. Moll believed this for as long as it had seemed true. But as a woman — as a mother — she knows there is suffering that transcends God himself.

The bread is on the fire and the baby is chewing at her breast. The new moon comes tomorrow night. Moll maps out paths in her head: the trail that runs from the quarters onto Asa's land, the garden path that sneaks from his wife's roses around the side of the house to the lawn, the channel between the mainland and the shoals, the unknown road to Wilmington. She draws these maps on her baby's back, and they are soothing. Moses is somewhere else, visiting a friend or a woman. She feeds the girls biscuits before bed, and they lie together until some of them fall asleep.

In the morning, she is in the fields again. She doesn't think of her son, or of the four hundred miles. She thinks of the dirt and the hoe and the seed, and in her break for dinner under the sweet gum tree, she thinks of the boat, practicing her strokes with open hands for oars. The afternoon turns warm, and the others sing while they plant — a low song, joyless. Abel works at the end of a row, his shirt off and the stripes on his back catching the sun. Her courage grows by the hour. She doesn't understand why so many of these people will never make the attempt. Why this land is such a sinkhole for human will. And yet: she is thirty-three years old, almost thirty-four, and has she ever tried to leave? Has freedom ever been something she would die to have? Even now, it's not freedom she's after. It's the boy, old enough to know the evils he's up against, too young to defend himself. You cannot take a child from its parent. Not when it's so young. Not when it's grown. The parent will walk until it is found again.

She is whipped once for resting. A line of blood rises on her arm.

When she gave birth to Davy, she was alone; her husband wasn't there, or the midwife, or Helen, who had once promised Moll a stock of childbed linen but who instead took to sea with a soldier in the middle of Moll's pregnancy. She gave birth in the dark, in an empty cabin, a rag between her teeth. He was a purple boy, then brown and warm and loud. A body that she had created from nothing: from abuse, from rotten corn, from forced labor. He had not a stain on him. She kissed him and brought him, still corded, to her breast. His face, his wrists, his toes. Faultless. Had her own mother loved Moll as much? She was a cipher, sold when Moll was just beginning to walk. Mothers fail

252

their children in so many ways. Not Moll. Not with this boy.

That night, she asks Moses to take the girls to Aunt Caty's cabin; she wants to drag the mattress out and scrub the floors. When they leave, she bundles up the sheets and carries the mattress and the stool and the pots and the cradle onto the porch. The only thing left, in the corner, is her bag. She tucks it under her arm and looks once around the room. Outside, the stars are just emerging. She takes no light with her. At the cabin next to hers, an old woman sits on the porch steps, braiding a child's hair.

Moll heads toward the creek; for anyone watching, she could be taking her clothes to wash. The darkness soon swallows her, and she begins to hurry. From Asa's pines, she can hear the trembling yelp of a nightjar. By the time she reaches his back garden, with its ripe smell of roses, the sky is patched with thin clouds. A light burns behind curtains in a second-floor window. She follows the line of the house, snaking around its brick corners, avoiding the gravel walkways. She stops beneath the curve of the front staircase to watch the lawn. It stretches like an open mouth to the sea. She waits until she is sure it's empty. The only person who ever walked the lawn at night was Helen; Moll used to watch her linger after supper, first as a girl enchanted by the ocean and starlight, and then as a woman waiting for a soldier. Helen must have thought her walks were secret, but she wasn't old enough, levelheaded enough, to wander without being watched. Perhaps Asa too sat on his bedroom floor and peered at his daughter from a corner of the upstairs window. They had let it happen. When Helen ran away, was either of them surprised? Moll has her own children to watch now; she can't bring herself to feel any guilt over Helen's fate. The circle of people she calls family narrows every year.

Moll skirts the lawn around its border, where a woman once planted rhododendrons. Untended, they have grown leggy and wild. Creeping along their edge, she feels the small whips of their branches on her face. The clouds have thickened, and their whiteness illuminates the new spring grass. Moll watches them, and goes more slowly. What will Moses do when he finds her gone? She sometimes visits with neighbors in the evening. Will he drag the mattress back in and fall asleep, or will he wait for her until he worries? He has never waited for her. She takes her time approaching the shore.

The rope is knotted in a strange, twisting hitch around the willow trunk. She can't see the ends, and it takes her a few minutes to fumble it free. She feels two drops of rain; they fall on the back of her neck and on her arm, just above the cut from the whip. She holds the loose rope in her hands and follows it down to the reeds, where she clutches the bow of the row-boat. The rain begins to sprinkle steadily. Moll throws her bag in and walks onto the clump of reeds, her feet half sinking, as she pushes the boat off into the clear water. Once it's free, she clambers in, getting wet almost to her knees. The rain pelts. She fumbles around the bottom of the boat, feeling for the oars, but her hands touch nothing. She gropes beneath the thwarts, in the bow, along the outside hull. She kicks her bag to one side. How big are oars? She retraces the lines of the boat, feeling now for sticks, flotsam. Nothing. The boat has rocked out into the channel now, pushed by the wind that carries the rain. It slowly turns, pointing toward the sandbar and the open ocean beyond. Moll digs her hand into the water on one side, but the sides of the boat are high, and she can only reach far enough for weak paddles. The boat continues to drift. She pauses, waits, looks out at the dark water surrounding the boat. In her cabin, the sound of the spring rain would help her children sleep.

She is still only a few yards from shore. Oars do not vanish. She leaves her bag in the boat and jumps into the cold water. She finds the line knotted to the bow and swims to the bank, dragging the boat behind her. The water is still shallow enough for her to find some footholds in the muck. She climbs into the reeds, onto the muddy ground. She leaves the boat resting half in the sea grass, its rope loose, and runs along the edge of the lawn to the outbuildings behind the house. There is a shed where Asa used to keep extra wood for barrels and his wife's dibbers and shears. Even after wiping the rain from her face, Moll can see nothing. She reaches out toward some tall shapes, and a scythe crashes to the floor. In the distance, a dog barks. She stops moving, thinks she hears a door shut in the big house. Alone in that house, is Asa afraid? Does he prowl the grounds at night, missing his family? She takes a step outside to see if the light in the house is moving. She sees a dark shape in the pines. Beneath the sound of the rain is a rustling. Feet. If they discovered her absence, who would be the first to come? The driver, with a gun? She runs back to the lawn, past the fringe of rhododendrons, down to the boat. She fumbles in it for her bag. She can no longer tell apart footsteps and the sound of water drumming on the boards. Will she die before she even begins?

She heads away from the noises, west, through the trees along the path to town. This is the way she would go if she had a boat and oars. Should she have taken the scythe, cut down branches from the willow to make paddles? She is frantic. She has made a mistake. She can see one of the tall lamps that light Front Street. When errors have been made, they must be forgotten. She slows her pace, holds her bag as if it were ordinary. Beaufort once had a slave patroller, but the town has shrunk since the war, and men are expected to protect their own property. She holds her head up and concentrates on taking even steps. The only people on the street are a few old men sitting on the stoop of the public house with glasses of beer. She smiles at them; one whistles. The bile is rising in her throat. To her left, she can see the boats bobbing by the docks. The men watch her progress. At the far end of town, she turns north. The street becomes a path again. The trees close in. She comes to the Newport River, which she cannot cross. She continues north along its bank, toward New Bern, the city to which all slaves run. Once they know she's missing, they can find her within an hour. From what Abel told her, the Newport swells into a wide bay before it becomes a creek again. There is no crossing west for eight or nine miles. If she can make it till daylight, she might have a chance.

Moll ties her skirt into a knot above her knees and begins to run.

The morning is wet and gray; the rain muffles the sound of the knock. Asa pushes back the covers and reaches for his robe. He stands at the window, waiting for the visitor to leave. A young man wearing a cap jogs down the stairs to his horse, which is stamping one hoof in a puddle. Asa crawls back into bed without removing his dressing gown.

His hunger wakes him. Downstairs, he lights a fire in the parlor and then descends to the kitchen for some bread and butter. In the dim light, he knocks against the oars leaning on the hearth. He had forgotten he had brought them inside for sanding. He would've done it in the shed, but it was too cold outside, and this room had a fireplace. He is glad there's no one to see his weaknesses. He runs his hand along the rough paddles. Maybe tomorrow, when the sun is out. He carries the half loaf and the small bowl of butter upstairs and eats on a stool beside the fire so the butter melts and his hands are warm.

He feels a nagging unhappiness and searches for its cause. Tab? John? No, he remembers: Moll. He is sorry that he couldn't please her. He has lost most of his fight, but he hasn't lost his sense of justice. You cannot simply free a slave because you love them in a way. There is an order to the human system; you are born in a certain stratum, and you work very hard with your hands and with your wits so that your children are wealthier, happier. You cannot just ask for favors. Asa's children would have had a better life, and this residual pride warms his chest. Moll too must earn that pride. Whether or not our children are taken away from us, we have a duty to God to be honest and uncomplaining. We cannot fight his will. This soothes Asa, and he finishes all of the bread, licking the butter off his fingers. He will not fight, and he will be rewarded. He curls on the rug by the fireplace and dozes.

In his dream, a bird is perched on his shoulder, nuzzling in his hair. He wakes, and the martin flutters to a corner of the ceiling, where it bats around before dipping down to knock against the glass. Asa must have left a window open before the rains came. He stands up slowly from the rug, one leg tingling, and limps to the dining room, leaning against the walls for support. He shuts the open window. The martin cannot seem to leave the parlor; Asa waits in the door and watches it fumble for an exit. Deep blue and sheeny, it would be a pretty bird to keep. Its panicked chirping sounds almost like a child. He could build a birdcage, teach it to eat crumbs from his hand. He finds the straw broom Mrs. Randolph left behind and flushes the martin into the hallway. It clutches at the cornice and waits, its chest heaving like a bellows. When Asa opens the front door, a letter falls from the handle onto the porch. This morning — the young man on the horse must have delivered it. He thought that might have been a dream.

Was the martin? He looks up: It's still there, panting, head cocked, waiting for the next attack. He lifts the broom and, after a few false tries, persuades the bird out the door, where it bangs once against the top of the porch before lighting out into the open air, a flash of metallic blue.

The letter is in an uncertain hand; the letters jumble over each other and lean in unusual ways. He returns to the fire to read it and to warm his hands again.

This is for my mother, it says at the top, with several notes of exclamation. He is confused, and feels still asleep.

I am well, & John is well. We had a rough time crossing & met lots of men and Indians. I shot a turkey by myself & John cooked it. They are not as many black folk here, one I met was already free, which is how I'll be soon. I get four dollars a week, just for carrying bags & now splitting logs for the house. It is almost done, just needs a roof. One room for John and one for me & we cook outside. There are other boys here same age & we swim tho' the water is twice as cold. I was surprised to see the mountains, but now they are regular to me. When I get free, I will build a house next to John & plant corn. He don't know if it grows here, but I said it would. We get plenty of rain. I know you was mad when I left, but now I figure you will be proud. You should see my arms, they are much bigger. You would like it here. Give a kiss to the baby & one for you. Your son always, Davy.

259

On the back are two lines from John. He is well and encloses some money to give to Moll toward her freedom. He promises to write again. Asa looks at the date: March 3. It has taken more than a month for this to reach them. The money, of course, is gone, taken by some post boy on the road. At least they are healthy, and Moll will be pleased to hear from her son. What an adventurous boy. There is certainly something easier about sons.

It is past noon, but Asa is still full from his breakfast. The rain has slackened. He puts on a broad hat and leather boots and tucks the letter into his coat, along with a ten-dollar note from his own money box. He is nervous about approaching the quarters alone, so he makes first for Cogdell's house, where he is welcomed by a dark woman in a white lace apron. He asks to see Moll, and she waits, as though he is about to say something else. He doesn't, so she says, "I'll get the master."

Cogdell is grim. He stands in the doorway rather than inviting Asa inside. "She's not here," he says.

"How's that?"

"Didn't show up in the fields this morning. Husband hadn't seen her. I was about to send over a note. She's yours, of course, but since I've been hiring her out for the past few years, figured I'd send my own men after her."

Asa concentrates. He had a conversation with her just yesterday, or maybe the day before, and the girl asked for her freedom. Now he has a letter for her, with a little money, that she'll be happy to receive. Where is she? Certainly nowhere that warrants men with guns and dogs. He doesn't remember her running away.

"No, no," he says, "that's all right." He reaches out for Cogdell's arm as a gesture of authority, but the tremor in his hand makes it seem instead like he is leaning on his neighbor. "I sent her on an errand. Asked her to get some things from New Bern."

Cogdell lowers his arms, forcing Asa to release his hand.

"John left in the fall, of course," Asa says, "and it's been hard without the help. Just a few things I couldn't get here. Some tools. She said I ought to ask you first, and I forgot. My own memory off to sea."

"You sent her to New Bern."

"New blades for the pine hacks. They do them better than the smithy here. No need to look for her."

"Did you send her on a horse?"

Asa is reaching the limits of his imagination. Would he have sent her on a horse? He nods slowly. The lies are building with surprising speed, and he cannot find their origin. "She might stay over with a cousin. I gave her a pass for two days."

"You did."

Asa puts his hand on the pocket where the letter is. "Just came by to make sure she got off all right. I'll send her over when she returns."

Cogdell digs his fingers through a rough blond beard. He is a broad man, and younger than Asa. "She'll be wet through," he says.

Asa shifts his feet, leaving damp patches on his neighbor's porch. He can no longer meet the man's eye. "Should've told you sooner. It's just my memory. No need to send anyone. My responsibility."

He hurries home.

He would not free her, and now she's stolen herself and will be caught and flayed or killed. Another child he abandoned. But this is not fair to himself; she was never his child, and he only obeyed his conscience. His urge to save her now is merely compassion for the guilty. If she had given some hint of her desperation, he could have counseled her. In his cold, empty house, Asa can think of a dozen wise phrases. He understands why holiness comes out of monasteries.

He would have told her there was grace in resignation. That happiness hard-earned was happiness twice over. That mortals have no eye for fate. That we are little chess pieces held by a glorious Hand. She would have shaken her head and wept and he would have put an arm around her and slowly they would have resigned themselves together. And now he can only wonder where she is. Vain to wonder. She is not his child. But still he reaches; still he is certain of his own responsibility.

All he can do is wait. He moves from room to room without sitting. He regrets now having chased the martin out. There are no longer any corners to hide in. He avoids the mirror in the dining room, Helen's miniature on the mantel, the windows that reflect back the ocean. He doesn't want to face himself. He takes the letter out of his coat and carries it to the fire. Crumples it, twists it, but can't bring himself to burn it. One day he will hear of her capture — or he will hear again from John, describing how she emerged from the mountains like a mother bear sniffing out her son.

He misses supper too, and falls asleep in a slouch on one of the parlor's armchairs.

It is half a year now & no word from you, but John says mail often goes lost. I think maybe you're still sore at me for leaving, but then I think no, you're my mother & would write me a letter no matter. I'm writing my address on this extra large so you can copy it out clear when you reply. There's a school here now, just started this fall, & I go some days with the white boys and learn numbers. Also longer words that you would like. Rudimentary. Deliverance. Unconscionable, which I can never spell right so I had to look it up just then. I want to be a storekeeper, so I study ciphering & John is teaching me how to keep books. There's a man here from New York, & he talks very highly of it, so that is where I will go. I'm more than halfway to freedom, since I've gotten some extra money doing jobs for the parson here, like teaching Sunday school to the smallest children. I knew you'd laugh at that. What do I know about Jesus? Well, I can read now, so I know a whole lot. They're good stories, so I just tell them in my own words, sometimes adding a twist or two. Such as I had old Jonah cut up that whale from the inside out instead of waiting for God to save him. I acted it out, flailing my hands around in the little church. All the children were so excited they sucked their thumbs. It made a much better story. By Christmas I expect I'll be free. John said he'd give me one of the mules, which are older than we thought, so it may be dead by then, but if not I'll ride up to New York. Would you like to come? I wouldn't mind, just tell me, I can come & get you, & anyone else who'd like to go, tho' they would have to fit on Cinder's back. I'll have a store & sell everything you can think of and become a rich man very soon. They'll put my name on buildings, DAVY!

When he's awakened by the morning sun and the smell of drying grass, Asa is ravenous. He finishes off the bread, mostly stale now, with a slather of molasses. He's still hungry, and thinks of the fishing pole in the shed that Helen used a few times as a girl. He will take the pole and the oars — he'll sand them another day — down to the boat and catch himself a meal. He needs to redeem himself.

The rain has called out the bluets, which bloom in starlike patches on the sloping lawn. Birds hover and dip down for worms, but Asa cannot tell from a distance if one of them is his martin. By the shore, the boat's rope around the willow has come undone; the dinghy bobs several yards out in the water, the knot in the rope having been caught in the reeds. If a little rain can dislodge such a stern knot, he should drag the boat onshore when not in use. He steps gingerly onto the beaten-down reeds and pulls the rope in, bringing the boat within reach. Once he has settled himself and his pole and his oars, he pushes out again. He heads west down the channel to town; he is still nervous about being carried away in a tide and having no one to call for. He reaches down to scoop out some of yesterday's rain with his hands. In the puddle floats a scrap of cloth, a rough white linen. Asa doesn't own any material so coarse, except for some old blankets Helen used to lay out in the chickens' coop. It must have blown in on the storm, a small piece of someone else's story. He is sentimental, so he squeezes the water from the scrap and ties it around his fishing pole. For luck.

It is Wednesday, and Front Street is busy with women and their baskets. Most of the fishermen are still out at their work, and Asa ties up along the dock without being observed. He stops first at the store, which looks like a strange mirror of something familiar. All the bones of the place are there: the shelves, the columns, the broad counter. But where the candies were now sit the skeins of yarn, and the flour has been moved to the back. Several new muskets hang behind the counter. Where are the candies now? He used to buy them for Tab. Asa asks the proprietor, a man who looks nothing like John, for a pouch of minnows for bait.

He should stop by the church. It's been several weeks since his last visit, even though Dr. Halling came again to preach in March. It had been raining, and Asa was reluctant to see him. The door is unlocked, and Asa walks to the front pew and sits. The light coming through the windows is almost blue. He doesn't know who to pray for. Those whom he would call beloved are now beyond his reach. He closes his eyes and tries to think of God. "Please," he says. He has arrived at the dregs of his life, and he is hoping to be guided out with grace.

In the cemetery, bright green runners of grass have started stretching across the dirt of his grand-daughter's grave. A stone marker is planted at its head, but nothing is written on it. He should pay the mason to carve something, but this was John's duty. At first, Asa thought there was a chance he'd return, that the Southwest Territory would be too cold or landlocked for him. But there is nothing left for him here.

Except look at this sweet grave. Asa places his hand on the warm ground. Think of what lies beneath this stone. What girl is curled in a barrel, her hair the color of the rum she floats in. She is still here, her fevered body finally cooled. And her mother, beneath the oak, laid out in a white gown ten years ago. Asa stands. On the other side of the church, close to the chancel wall, his own wife sleeps. A garden of women. He built Long Ridge for them, and they never came to claim it.

Moll too has left something for her son. Even if she is captured halfway to New Bern, she leaves an imprint of action that the boy will one day learn of. All Asa has done is accumulate. He has waited for his visions to bear fruit, and in the waiting, generations of the young and lively have sailed into the world with blind trust. Who is he to bestow freedom?

266

He will talk to Cogdell about selling the rest of the acres. They are worthless to him. A man without an heir is an absence — an almost-man. Better to submit wholly now to what is left.

The fishing rod is still in his boat when he returns to the harbor, the tie of coarse linen fluttering. He rows into the sound, his stomach more accustomed to the roll of the waves. The water is gray and blue and darkens as its bottom sinks away. He is out of the narrow creek, has slipped through the sandbars into the deeper water. Bogue Island and Shackleford Banks rise up on either side — the last solid ground before the ocean. This is the farthest he's ever been from land. In the hollow between the great shoals, he pulls his oars in. His daughter and his granddaughter had seen this view and were not afraid. He has to believe they were not afraid.

He opens the bag of minnows. Some are already dead; others still thrash in the damp sacking. He reaches for his pole and discovers he didn't bring a hook for his line. He is relieved. He takes a few of the minnows in his hand and sprinkles them on the water. He waits, and soon a larger fish rises to circle beneath them. The sun is beginning to drift toward the horizon. Its light cuts from the west and catches the lip of the waves and the white fish bellies. Mackerel and sheepshead gather, and the minnows disappear. When the feast is over, the fish slide away, leaving the dark water blank again. Asa could keep rowing, past the banks into the bottomless ocean, could grieve without witnesses, could surrender his body to the unseen. But he is hungry, and is sorry now not to have caught a fish. He turns the boat again toward shore. The sea will be here in the morning.

Author's Note

Parts of this novel are based on actual historical events, and several characters have borrowed the names of real people. These facts have been gently muddled to suit the narrative's needs. For those interested in learning more about the history of this area, Charles L. Paul's thesis "Colonial Beaufort: The History of a North Carolina Town" (1965) is an excellent place to start.

Acknowledgments

This book is a product of the Bennington Writing Seminars, where I finally grew into myself. My classmates, my workshop mates, my dance partners — this book is theirs.

I would like to acknowledge that David Gates, Amy Hempel, and Jill McCorkle are among the most generous of human beings, and that Bret Anthony Johnston and Paul Yoon are family to me, and beloved. I also owe a debt to my biological family. I have yet to deserve them.

I want to thank Bill Clegg for being a classic superhero and Terry Karten for being my ideal shepherd. I am endlessly grateful to be part of this business of imagination.

THE BIRDCAGE

Clive Aslet

Salonika, 1916: a city that is nominally neutral, but is teeming with French, British, and Serbian armies. A city seething with intrigue, where the native inhabitants are eager to make what money they can from the foreign soldiery. Welcome to the Birdcage, named after the miles of tangled barbed wire separating the city from the fighting to the North. It is the Casablanca of WWI. This kaleidoscope of nations, cultures and political ambitions shifts and re-forms around a group of English men and women, blown there by many different winds — into a world of madcap journeys by mule, motor car, and foot over the grim mountains; of U-boats lurking in the waters; of the sinister Gazmend Effendi. What is his game? Where is all the petrol disappearing to? The breathless ride is just beginning . . .

EXPOSURE

Helen Dunmore

London, November, 1960: The Cold War is at its height. Spy fever fills the newspapers, and the political establishment knows how and where to buy its secrets. When a highly sensitive file goes missing, Simon Callington is accused of passing information to the Soviets, and arrested. His wife, Lily, suspects that his imprisonment is part of a cover-up, and that more powerful men than Simon will do anything to prevent their own downfall. She knows that she too is in danger, and must fight to protect her children. But what she does not realise is that Simon has hidden vital truths about his past, and may be found guilty of another crime that carries with it an even greater penalty . . .

A PERFECT HOME

Kate Glanville

Claire appears to have it all — the kind of life you read about in magazines: a beautiful cottage, three gorgeous children, a handsome husband in William, and her own flourishing vintage textile business. But when an interiors magazine sends a good-looking photographer to take pictures of Claire's perfect home, he makes her wonder if the house means more to William than she does, and question whether home really is where the heart is . . .

YANTO'S SUMMER

Ray Pickernell

Post-war Gloucestershire: Yanto Gates, invalided out of the Army towards the end of the war, enjoys civilian life in the small village of Purton East, but he misses the thrill and risk of combat. He's had to readjust to a sedate life of dock work, fishing, and "going steady" — but things don't stay that way for long, especially not when an old flame of his returns to a nearby town. There are dark secrets and old feuds at play in this sleepiest of villages . . .